GOODBYE, MY LOVE

Vanessa Sanderson, betrayed by the man she loves, wants to distance herself from the heartache. So she escapes to Brae, a remote Scottish island. When the darkly attractive Robert McKenzie enters her life, the islanders close in to protect him. What are they hiding? Vanessa becomes wary of Robert's advances while she tries to discover the reason for the secrecy. Will the islanders let her help them, or will Robert force her to leave before her plans are complete?

JEAN ROBINSON

GOODBYE, MY LOVE

Complete and Unabridged

LINFORD
Leicester

First published in Great Britain in 2009

First Linford Edition
published 2012

British Library CIP Data

Robinson, Jean.
   Goodbye, my love. - -
   (Linford romance library)
   1. Love stories.
   2. Large type books.
   I. Title II. Series
   823.9′2–dc23

   ISBN 978–1–4448–1363–0

Published by
F. A. Thorpe (Publishing)
Anstey, Leicestershire

Set by Words & Graphics Ltd.
Anstey, Leicestershire
Printed and bound in Great Britain by
T. J. International Ltd., Padstow, Cornwall

This book is printed on acid-free paper

The Isle of Brae Beckons

As an enormous wave lashed the boat, Vanessa gripped the edge of the wooden plank seat to prevent herself from ending up in the bottom of the boat amidst salt water and fishing tackle.

Water dripped down the collar of her waterproof jacket but at least her feet were warm and dry in the wellies her mother had insisted she wear.

'Does it ever stop raining up here?' she shouted above the roar of the wind.

'We don't come here for the weather, dear,' Audrey Sanderson said. The neat little woman was perched on a lobster pot, clad in waterproofs from head to foot.

'But, Mum, it's May, supposed to be spring. It was lovely yesterday in Brighton. I was sitting out in the sun.'

'And it can be very nice up here at times. Your dad and I have had some lovely weeks in these islands over the years. But on the west coast of Scotland you do have to expect more rain.'

A smile touched Vanessa's lips as she glanced up at the wheelhouse. The boatman was steering his course through the rough sea, his dark curly hair ruffled with wind and rain, the collar of his waterproof jacket turned up round the polo-necked sweater he wore. She couldn't see his face clearly through the salt-spattered glass but it was firmly imprinted on her mind: brown eyes, fine features, a strong jaw-bone and sensitive mouth.

They had been bouncing around on this rough sea since leaving Mallaig an hour ago. From the moment he had taken her hand to help her down from the quay and his smiling eyes had held hers for just a second, she had felt a definite lift in her mood.

'Vanessa, come up here,' her father shouted above the roar of the engine. She struggled over a variety of obstacles and climbed the ladder into the small space where the two men were standing. At least in the wheelhouse there was some shelter from the elements.

Her father was trying to make out the various islands and mountains, but it was the boatman she was interested in, those deep dark eyes which had just glanced at her and the smile that turned her legs to jelly.

He was steering his course through the waves, his large frame dwarfing the small space; head lowered to peer out through the spray which splattered the glass.

Her father was swaying naturally with the movement of the boat, oblivious to the water dripping down over his eyes from his ancient sou'wester.

'How many years have you worn that hat, Dad?' Vanessa laughed.

'Don't you mock, my girl, this hat is keeping me dry. Better than the stuff you can buy these days,' Geoff Sanderson retorted.

Again her eyes were being drawn to

the boatman, his broad hands on the wheel, weather-beaten face scanning the horizon. Quickly she turned away and tried to make out the various landmarks her father was pointing to.

'But I can hardly see a thing,' she groaned peering through the swirling mist.

'You can if you know what to look for.'

The boatman's voice was soft and cultured with just a hint of his native land.

'Yes, well, that's true, but as I haven't been here before, I don't.' Why did she feel so irritable?

'You sound as if you need this holiday.' Again with the briefest of glances, the dark eyes held hers.

'I'm tired and I'm cold and I want the sun to shine.' It sounded pathetic as soon as she'd said it and she was annoyed at herself now for being so prickly. The stress of the last months was taking its toll and he was right, she did need this holiday.

'You'd be warmer down below. There's some hot coffee in a flask.'

'That would be lovely,' she said, and eased herself down into the small cabin, grateful to escape temporarily from the wind.

It was cosy and clean with a bunk to one side and a tiny porthole above it. A large chart was spread over half the table with a thermos flask and a box of sandwiches on a shelf behind.

Warming her hands round a mug of coffee she braced herself against the bulkhead, sipping slowly, the hot liquid soothing and warming. The thick blanket on his bunk looked inviting and she realised how tired she was after the long journey.

There were clothes pushed under the bunk and seaman's boots in the middle of the floor. Then her eyes were drawn to a photo in a small gilt frame. Putting her mug down on the table she moved close to where it hung on the bulkhead just above his pillow, a pretty woman holding a small boy.

5

Why did her heart suddenly plummet? So he was married. So what? The last thing she wanted now was another man in her life. Slowly she sank on to the bed, leant back on a saggy cushion and let her mind drift back over the last few weeks. She missed Greg even though he had treated her badly. Here she was at twenty-six, love life in tatters, career on hold. Would this holiday with her parents on a remote Scottish island really help her to sort it all out?

'Vanessa, are you all right down there?'

Her father's voice brought her back to the present and she climbed slowly back on deck. The clouds were thinning now showing large patches of blue sky, and round her, mountain ranges rose from a calmer sea.

She slipped off her jacket and enjoyed the feel of May sunshine on her arms. Geoff made his way unsteadily down the ladder to join her mother, and a stab of pain touched her as she saw how frail her father had become since his heart attack.

The boatman smiled at her, a smile that crinkled the corners of his eyes. 'Well, are you happy now? I've organised the sunshine for you. Make the best of it for it won't last long.'

She smiled back and held her face to the sun.

'We're coming up to the island now. There it is, the Isle of Brae,' he said with pride.

In the distance she could just make out the rocky coastline glinting green in the sunlight. Swirling round its higher peaks was a wispy mist as if teasing and giving the whole a mystical quality.

'Misty Island,' she whispered to herself and was aware of his eyes upon her again.

'Misty Island,' he repeated. 'I like that.'

She watched the swirling mist round the peaks and listened to his soft voice.

'You can see for miles from the top on a clear day.'

'And do you have clear days?'

'Only in July,' he responded.

'But, I won't be here in July!'

'Then, I'm afraid you'll miss out.'

He was enjoying teasing her so she nudged him playfully, but when her arm touched his it was electrifying. Every nerve in her body tingled. She quickly moved away and he became more serious too.

'And what bring you to these islands?'

Struggling to gain her composure she said, 'Oh, I'm just the chauffeur. Dad's not been too well lately and Mum doesn't drive. They love these islands so I thought the holiday would do them good.'

'It's a long drive. You should have got the train.'

'Yes, I suppose that would have made sense, especially as we weren't able to bring the car over to the island.'

'I'm afraid the harbour is too small for car ferries.'

'I'm happy to leave it in Mallaig. I've had enough driving just getting here.'

'And what do you do for a living?' He

was just making polite conversation but she really didn't want to go down this route.

'My last job was designing theatre props and acting with a small company in Brighton.'

'You work in a theatre?'

'I did, until last week.'

Greg's blue-grey eyes still haunted her, his startling good looks and wildly artistic temperament.

'We used to produce a play every couple of months, work with children in local schools, take our plays to other towns.'

'So what went wrong?'

She felt her throat tighten. 'Oh, emotions getting in the way of work, lots of factors. Anyway I'm moving on after this break.'

'So what next?'

'I don't know. I've had some offers. I'd like to get into producing eventually. When I get back I'll look into all the possibilities. At the moment I just want to relax.'

They stood in companionable silence as he let the boat drift along the rugged coastline towards the jetty.

★   ★   ★

'Robert McKenzie seems nice and friendly,' Audrey commented when Vanessa joined her mother back on the deck. 'Dad says he lives on the island. Can you believe there are only a hundred and twenty-three people living there? Robert says it's the most peaceful place on earth. I'm so glad we decided to come here instead of going back to Skye or Rhum. It is nice to explore new places and I hadn't even heard of Brae before.'

'It looks quite magical with the mist hanging over it,' Vanessa mused.

'You look better already, dear. Three weeks on the island will do you no end of good. Get some roses back in your cheeks.'

Her mother was right. Drawing fingers through her dark curly hair to tease out the tangles, she watched the coastline getting ever nearer and felt more peaceful than she had for a long time.

★ ★ ★

Robert felt his heart lift as the boat came nearer and nearer to the island. His hand rested lightly on the wheel as he brought them in towards the jetty and he found it difficult to take his eyes off Vanessa as she stood talking to her mother. There was something about the girl, her look, the way she moved, the hurt in her eyes when they'd talked about whatever it was she was escaping from. Something was stirring inside him; something he hadn't felt for a very long time, thought he would never feel again.

He gripped the wheel more tightly and focused his mind on the task in hand. He must put all this nonsense out of his mind.

Robert drove them to Dove Cottage

and helped them unload in a downpour of rain.

'Never mind, dear, we'll soon have a nice big fire in that grate and it'll be cosy and warm. You go and have a lie down while Dad and I sort things out. You must be worn out after driving all day.'

Even though the bed felt cold and damp she was glad to stretch out and let her mind drift, and it drifted back to Robert McKenzie.

★   ★   ★

When she ventured back into the living room an hour later her mother had it cosy with a log fire blazing and a hot dinner on the table. Then they sat on the chintzy covered easy chairs reading and dozing until the light began to fade.

'We'd better get to bed soon,' her father said. 'No electricity here, you know. Up with the lark and to bed before dark.'

'What, you mean we don't have any

lights.' Vanessa could not believe what she was hearing.

'Only gas, fiddling to light and not very effective. I'll have a go if you want me to.'

Audrey yawned. 'No, don't bother tonight, Geoff. We're all tired. Vanessa, here, can hardly keep her eyes open.'

She was right. Not wanting to face the chilly bedroom, Vanessa snuggled up in her quilt on the hearthrug and was grateful just to be warm and dry. She was vaguely aware of her mother easing a pillow under her head and tucking the quilt more securely round her. It was good to be with them again.

★   ★   ★

Next day, when Vanessa dodged outside Dove Cottage during a lapse in the incessant rain to fetch in some logs for the fire, she was convinced it never stopped raining on this island, and that they would be cooped up inside for the entire three weeks. Yet looking out over the bay, even through misty rain, it was a beautiful place. Sea birds swooped and dived amongst the rocky outcrops, their call echoing through the air as grey sea and sky merged to form a background to the dark rocks and silver sands.

She shivered, pulling her cardigan closer round her for warmth and, lifting a bundle of logs, made her way back in.

'Just put them down on the hearth,' Audrey called from the kitchen. 'We'll soon have them blazing then I'll make us some lunch.'

'I'd like to go out for a while, Mum, if you don't mind. I'm not really hungry just yet.'

'All right, dear, but you're going to get wet.'

'I think it's easing now, Mum, so I'll take my chance whilst the going's good.'

'Good idea. I'm only making soup so I'll leave yours in the pan. You enjoy your walk. The fresh air will do you good. Dad and I may take a stroll later so we'll leave the back door on the latch. No need to lock up on this island. I don't think we even have a door key.'

The road followed the bay round and then veered off towards the centre of the island through a wide valley between towering mountains.

The sky began to lighten and the mist rose to show further heights of crazy peaks. On the gentler slopes of the valley the grass was rich for grazing and scattered with sheep. A stream ran beside the road, its banks a nestling place for tiny wild flowers of delicate shade, the damp air pungent with wild garlic. Bluebells grew in profusion under the trees in a copse and she stopped to listen to the birdsong.

'It's a bullfinch,' a voice said softly from behind her.

Vanessa spun round and the small bird she had been idly watching left its perch on the fencing post and flew off into the depth of the wood.

Robert McKenzie grinned down at her, his dark eyes laughing at her surprise.

'I didn't hear you drive up,' she said.

'You were in a world of your own. The island has that effect on people.'

Taking an axe from the back of his truck, he ambled through the gate into the wooded area and began to chop at the segments of a felled tree.

She watched him steadily reduce it into a pile of logs and then to load them into a wheelbarrow, his muscular arms making light work of it. When he looked up at her she realised how rudely she had been staring at him.

'I'm sorry, I'm just fascinated by how easily you can do that.'

'I'm used to it,' he shrugged. 'You can help if you want to; load while I chop.'

'I'm not sure I'll be able to keep up with you.'

His answering smile reassured her, so she wandered over and began to fill the barrow, all the time conscious of his nearness. When his arm touched hers as they worked together she felt the excitement rising again.

16

They continued for about half an hour in companionable silence. Suddenly he stopped, helped her load the last few and threw the axe into the back of the truck.

'You did well,' he said, and she smiled, thinking how much she had enjoyed working with him.

'Like a lift back?' he asked.

Gratefully she accepted and heaved herself up into the truck.

'Don't mind if I deliver these first, do you?' he asked as they trundled along the rough road towards the other side of the island. 'Maude Campbell cleans my cottage so I deliver her logs.'

She shrugged. 'My time's my own.'

He turned to look at her. 'Do I detect a hint of boredom? It can't be much fun stuck here with your parents, away from the bright lights.'

'On the contrary. I really don't see enough of my parents these days and I've had enough of bright lights for a bit.'

If only she could stop thinking about

Greg, get him right out of her mind. They'd been together for two years, through all the ups and downs of running the small theatre. She missed the warmth of his touch, his easy laughter, the familiarity of his companionship.

Robert was studying her intently. 'So what about this Greg chap? I think he meant a lot to you. Is he the boyfriend you're running away from?'

How did he know all this? He must have heard it from her father when they were talking on the boat.

'I'm not running away from anyone. If you really must know he was the one who did the running.'

Here she was again, telling him things he really had no business knowing.

'I don't want to talk about it. It's too painful,' she snapped at him.

He gave her a sideways glance and they drove on for a while in silence.

'What about you?' she asked eventually. 'Don't you find it quiet on such a tiny island so far from land?'

He slapped on the brakes and came to a halt outside a large stone built house with hens in the yard and sheep scuttling up the hillside away from the truck.

'I'll just get Maude's logs unloaded,' he said, ignoring her question.

A tall thin middle aged woman stood at the door talking to Robert while he loaded the logs into her shed. She glanced occasionally in Vanessa's direction and gave her a hard stare before resuming her conversation with Robert and Vanessa had the uncomfortable feeling she was being talked about.

Robert continued stacking logs while the woman continued to stare at her, then they exchanged a few more words and Robert climbed back into the truck.

'She didn't look very friendly,' Vanessa commented.

'Maude's all right, it's just her way. I don't suppose these island people are quite what you're used to.'

She laughed at his assumption. 'What do you mean? What sort of people do you think I'm used to?'

'Well, showbiz people are different, aren't they? The artistic temperament and all that. People here are down to earth. They work hard just to survive on this island.'

She bristled. 'I work hard too. Acting is very hard work.'

He looked at her, grinning ruefully. 'Yes, I'm sure it is.'

She was silent, annoyed but not wanting an argument with him.

He turned to her. 'I'm sorry. Now I've upset you.'

She shrugged. What did it matter what he thought of her? Yet somehow it did matter.

They drove in an uncomfortable silence for a while. The road headed on across the island and suddenly dropped down to the far coast, which appeared more rugged than the gentler slope beneath Dove Cottage.

He stopped the truck on a precipice

overlooking a bay of silver sand ridged where the sea had ebbed. Black-headed gulls screeched and swooped and grey clouds gathered on the horizon.

'I thought you might like to see the view. It's the finest on Brae,' he said.

Vanessa shivered, not certain whether it was the sudden chill in the air or the closeness of the man beside her, a hair's breadth between his arm and hers.

He sensed her chill and looked at her with concern. 'You need warmer clothes up in these islands.'

'OK, so I don't have the right clothes and I'm just a temperamental actress. What else? Maybe I am different.'

He raised his hands in mock defence. 'Why are you so prickly? I didn't mean to offend; I'm just concerned for your comfort. There's a fleece in the back there if you want it.'

She gave him an apologetic look. 'Sorry, yes I could do with another layer. I do have the warm clothes. I'm just not used to wearing them as it's so much warmer down on the south coast.'

He climbed out and came round to open the door for her, then took her hand to help her down, holding it a little longer than was necessary.

Standing side by side at the cliff's edge they watched together as waves lapped the beach, circling great boulders like islands.

'It's a beautiful sight,' she said softly.

'We could drop down on to the beach and walk along a little way if you like,' he offered.

'Yes, I'd like to, that's if you have time. I mean I don't want to keep you from your work.'

'I don't have any timetable,' he said, leading the way down a rugged path. When he turned to steady her, his touch held an unexpected warmth. 'My time's my own and I spend it how I please.'

Something just didn't add up here. Despite his workman-like clothes this young man seemed too refined and educated to be eking out a living on such a small island.

It was a difficult scramble and her

feet hurt through the thin canvas shoes.

'However do you manage to get clothes here?' she asked.

'You don't need many, so long as they are the right sort.'

Then he turned his dark eyes on her with a hint of humour and she realised he was teasing.

'I'm afraid the only shop on the island is the general store where Fiona stocks food and some essentials. Angus goes across in the boat once a week for supplies and often takes a passenger or two for shopping.'

'I can't imagine not being able to buy whatever I wanted at any time.'

'No, I can see that. You're a very sophisticated young lady.'

They walked side by side along the beach in companionable silence each wrapped in their own thoughts.

How different this calm, self-contained man was from the vibrant Greg. Greg would have told his whole dramatic life story by now yet she knew nothing of Robert.

'Don't you feel a bit cut off here on such a tiny island?' she asked.

There was a long pause then he stopped and stared out to sea again, his eyes focussing on some distant point. 'Yes, but it's the way I like it,' he said, as if to himself. Then he turned to her. 'I imagine you have many friends.'

'Yes, Brighton's a lively place, lots of clubs and great places to eat. I'd be lost without my friends.'

'Yes, I think you would.'

Large drops of rain began to drop from a heavily laden sky and he grabbed her hand and quickly pulled her up the beach into a large cave in the rocky coast.

'Not rain again,' she groaned, relieved that the tension was broken.

He laughed heartily for the first time and his eyes took on a special magic.

'How long are you here for?' he asked.

'Three weeks, maybe longer. Dad retired from teaching last summer after his heart attack. He was due to retire soon anyway. It just brought things forward a bit. I don't have any commitments at the moment so we can stay as long as we like.'

'They sound a devoted couple, your parents. Do you have any brothers or sisters?'

'No, just me. They had me late in life after they had established their careers.'

'An only child, then?'

'Yes, but we did lots together as a family and my friends were always welcome. I just wish I could spend more time with them now.'

'So why not?'

'My work takes me away from home. There aren't too many theatres in a small Sussex village.'

He was still smiling his infectious smile. 'And now you've ended up on a windswept island. Didn't your parents prepare you for this?'

She nodded. 'Yes, they told me. I just couldn't believe anywhere could be so primitive.'

She could see she'd hurt his feelings.

'Natural is the word,' he said, serious again.

She tried quickly to make amends. 'Yes, I'm sorry, it is very beautiful.' She meant it, too. Even with rain falling, the grey splendour of it, looking out from their shelter, was awe-inspiring.

'How did you know this cave was here?' she asked.

'There are plenty of caves along this coast. There are stories, too, about massacres in days gone by and how clans hid in these caves to escape attack from other islands. The bones of many people were found in one cave not so long ago and were reckoned to have been there for several hundred years. I'll tell you about them one day, but the tales need to be told on a dark night round a log fire. It gives more atmosphere.'

He stood so close she could feel his breath on her neck and began to visualise sitting with Robert round a log fire on a dark night.

Then she forced herself to remember the photo of the woman and child in his cabin on the boat, and concentrated her mind on the scenery and the rain, aware that she should not be here with him at all.

Robert obviously had the same thoughts. 'The rain's easing now. I think we should get back,' he said, and they made their way along the beach to where the path led up to the truck.

It was a bumpy ride back and Robert made no allowance for the uneven road.

By the time he drew up at Dove Cottage it was mid afternoon and the sun shone brightly. She jumped down and thanked him for the ride.

'There's a ceilidh tonight. Would you like to come?'

She looked doubtful.

'It's in the ceilidh hall, up the road and over the hill, near the church,' he told her. 'It'll be starting about seven. There'll be lots of people there, all the locals and most of the summer visitors. You'll enjoy it and get to know people.' His mouth turned into a broad smile and his eyes held hers for a moment.

She smiled back. 'Sounds fun.'

He waved and she watched as his truck trundled back up the road then she pushed open the cottage door and called out, 'I'm back and I'm starving. I hope you've saved me some soup.'

Her mother was giving her a strange look and she realised she had walked into the cottage grinning.

Robert was thoughtful as he drove back to his cottage. Why had he done that? Why had he asked her to the ceilidh? He was sending out all the wrong signals, giving the impression he was interested in her. He had to get a grip on himself.

Vanessa Attends The Ceilidh

'How does one dress for a ceilidh?' she asked her mother as she sifted through a selection of cotton skirts and thin blouses.

'Remember you have to walk there and back,' Audrey warned. 'And it does get chilly in the evenings.'

Eventually she decided on a simple summer dress and flat patent leather shoes.

As she set off for the hall she wondered how she would fit in, a woman on her own not knowing anyone, and she did have to stifle the slight uneasiness that she may be going to this dance just to see Robert again.

The entire island seemed to be present with babies gurgling from pushchairs in corners, and tiny tots jumping around riotously.

The band, made up of local talent, consisted of bagpipes, fiddles and a selection of brass played at full volume, the bearded pipe player lubricating his tubes with frequent slurps from a whisky bottle.

When Robert saw her standing on her own watching, he danced his way out of a complicated reel and, still holding on to his partner, wove through the dancers towards her.

'This is Fiona and that's Angus and Dougal,' he said pointing out as many people nearby as he could and they all nodded in acknowledgment.

Then cakes and sandwiches were being brought round by the children and mugs of tea. It was a wooden hall with a tin roof and benches to sit on and Vanessa couldn't help comparing it with the sophistication she had left behind and felt a pang of longing for Greg and their intimate suppers of French cuisine.

Suddenly her reverie was broken and she was being drawn on to the floor by

Angus, the bearded pipe player, all her protestations ignored. He had rough hands and a coarse shirt, his accent totally beyond her comprehension.

As they twisted and turned to the ever faster and louder music she concentrated hard to remember some basic steps from her country dancing days at school. Soon she was hot and winded and wanted only to collapse on one of the wooden benches with a cold drink.

'You're here on holiday then?' a plump lady beside her said in a high pitched voice.

Vanessa turned and saw a friendly face with grey hair drawn into a bun and hands poised over an ample bust.

'I'm Hettie McPhearson and I teach up at the school. You'd be passing the school with Robert this afternoon.'

'Yes, I remember, it seemed very tiny,' Vanessa said.

'Why, yes, we have only twelve children there. Then they must go away back to the mainland for their secondary education. You could maybe pop in and see us one day when you're settled in, maybe do a wee bit of acting with the little ones. I hear you're an actress yourself,' Hettie continued.

'That's right,' she agreed, surprised at how fast gossip travelled in a small community like this. Her mind was only half on the conversation because she was busy watching Robert swinging his partner down the set, hands crossed and smiling.

'You've an eye for Robert, I see,' Hettie said, following her gaze.

Vanessa flushed scarlet.

'He's a fine, handsome man is Robert. You'll not be the first to fall for his charm,' Hettie continued.

'Yes, he's very nice,' Vanessa stuttered.

'Many a girl has been taken in by that smile. He's too handsome for his own good, is our Robert.'

Vanessa recovered enough to try to deflect any ideas Hettie might have about her and Robert.

'He doesn't seem to be having any

problems at the moment,' she laughed.

Hettie became more serious. 'No, dear, not at the moment.'

He really was the most handsome man in the hall, in fact the most handsome man she had ever set eyes on. His wife was a lucky lady.

'Which one's his wife?' she asked Hettie, trying to make it sound casual.

'Och, dear, he doesn't have a wife now.'

Vanessa felt a flood of relief wash over her.

'What happened?' she ventured.

Hettie gave her a philosophical smile. 'It's a sad story. The poor lad's had a bad time. I doubt he'll ever get over it completely.'

Vanessa gave her a questioning look, not sure she should press any further. Hettie patted her knee. 'Now, don't you worry your head about it. But don't go falling for our Robert or you'll only get hurt.'

She didn't feel she could pursue this conversation. What did it matter anyway, their worlds were miles apart? But her eyes sought him out involuntarily.

Hettie followed her gaze, then looked back at her with a quizzical look, but kept her thoughts to herself.

The hall was becoming hot and noisy and though everyone seemed friendly, Vanessa was feeling a little left out.

The music stopped and everyone dispersed from the floor.

'Why, now it's a waltz,' Hettie said. 'I used to like to waltz with my Bertie. Spin round the floor, we did.' A dreamy look came over her.

'But the music's very fast for a waltz,' Vanessa said. 'And they're dancing a different step.'

'Och, it's only a slight variation. You'll soon get the hang of it. And here's your young man come to sweep you off your feet,' she teased.

Robert was standing in front of her offering his hand. 'Will you dance with me?'

She looked up into his smiling brown eyes and knew she wanted to more than anything.

'I'm not sure that I can manage those steps,' she said.

'You'll be fine,' he reassured her.

Immediately she found herself enfolded in strong arms. As he held her firmly and guided her round the floor she easily followed his strong lead and quickly fell into the rhythm. His skin was flushed with dancing and his curly hair fell over his forehead. Relaxing in his arms she no longer felt alone.

She could feel his breath on her neck, his tightening grip round her waist and the hard muscular strength of his body.

The music stopped and he gave her a final twirl and then led her back to her seat.

'Now, you looked just a picture, the two of you swirling round together,' Hettie said. 'Robert cuts a fine figure on the dance floor, and you're very graceful, my dear. I expect it's with being an actress.'

'I have had a lot of training in dance and I love the music.'

'Why, yes, it's a cheerful sound they

make between them. Angus gets better as the whisky bottle empties.' They both laughed.

Sets were grouping now for the next dance and Robert was coerced by a small group to complete their number.

'Now, here comes Angus again,' Hettie said.

Vanessa needed to take her mind off Robert so at the end of the next dance she went to talk to some of the summer visitors who were gathered in a corner of the hall.

When another waltz was announced an involuntarily spark of excitement shot through her, but it was quickly extinguished when she saw Robert scoop another young woman into his arms.

Hettie was at her side again. 'I'm just leaving now, dear. Would you like to come in the car with me? I could drop you off on the way.'

She thanked her gratefully, suddenly feeling very tired and not wanting the long walk home alone.

Retrieving her coat from the cloak-room was an obstacle course over tiny bodies sleeping soundly on the floor beneath blankets, safely snug in their own little world.

As she stepped out into the night suddenly Robert was beside her. He took her arm and guided her to the waiting car.

'I hope you enjoyed the ceilidh.'

'Yes, it was fun,' she said.

'Would you like me to show you some more of the island tomorrow? We could take a picnic and explore the northern end. There are eagles nesting up there and we'll maybe find some seals in the bay. Or do you have other plans?'

'No, that would be lovely,' she said without thinking. But what was the harm in it? He wasn't married and was obviously unattached or he wouldn't be asking her, and Hettie hadn't seemed to disapprove of her dancing with him.

The journey home in Hettie's car was magical.

'Look, Hettie, how the moon is illuminating the bay and how the sea sparkles silver.'

'Yes, it's a fine night,' Hettie said with satisfaction.

Her heart was light with anticipation and warm still with the memory of Robert's arms around her and the rhythm of a Scottish waltz dancing in her ears.

Robert stayed outside, reluctant to return to the crowded hall. He felt at peace here in the moonlight, surrounded by the dark mountains and the fresh night air. And he felt close to her, the feel of her in his arms, the way she danced, her smiling eyes. Then a twist of hurt made him grimace. She didn't belong here. Hers was a different life in a different place. He could never have her, even if he wanted to. And he knew, more than anything, that he wanted to.

* * *

Vanessa woke next morning to a brilliant blue sky and the promise of a warm, summer day. She pulled back chintzy curtains and watched the sheep scatter from the grassy slope which fronted their cottage, the tiny lambs following closely, afraid to be separated from their mothers.

The sound of the sea breaking on the jutting rocks surrounding the bay floated through the open window. A fishing boat made its way back towards the harbour surrounded by gulls swooping and diving in hope of an easy breakfast.

'No need for waterproofs and jumpers today,' Audrey called from the kitchen where she was busy making sandwiches.

Vanessa went in and put the kettle on.

'We're off to Burren today. It's high in the cliffs where there's supposed to be a corncrake. It's a bird we've never seen before, they're very rare these days,' Audrey said.

'How will you get there?' Vanessa enquired.

'Robert popped in this morning before you were up, said he'd drive us over.

He's such a nice man.'

Vanessa panicked. 'He could be here any minute and I'm not even dressed yet.'

'Then, get yourself ready, dear. We don't want to keep him waiting. And don't worry, we don't expect you to stay with us all day. Robert said he was taking you sight-seeing then he'd pick us up later.'

* * *

She had just managed to squeeze into a pair of jeans when there was a screech of brakes on the path and a car door slammed.

'Are you right, then?' Robert asked, smiling on the doorstep.

His tall figure was framed in the doorway and, as her eyes took in the cream shirt which showed his muscular chest and tanned arms, a shiver of excitement surged through her.

'You don't give a girl much warning,' she laughed.

He looked surprised. 'You knew I was coming.'

'But I didn't know when. I might still have been in bed.'

'Och, we don't worry about time here,' he said. 'Not within an hour or so.'

His comfortable old car climbed the slope steadily over the clifftop, dropped her parents off with all their gear then trundled down into the next bay.

'It was fine out there this morning,' he told her, nodding towards the sea. 'I got a good catch, too.'

'You mean you've been fishing already this morning.'

'I do most mornings.'

'How wonderful. I'd like to go fishing sometime. Could you teach me to fish?' She was amazed at her boldness.

'No,' he said abruptly, and she immediately realised she had over-stepped the mark. But the change in his tone surprised her. His face was hard, the lines of his jaw set and he took a bend in the road faster than she

41

thought prudent. 'It's no place for women,' he said severely.

She laughed at his chauvinistic attitude, but the quiet intensity of his manner made her lay off any further argument. They were silent for a moment, and then she glanced at him, trying to weigh up his mood.

'I enjoyed the ceilidh last night,' she said, and he relaxed.

'There's very little in the way of entertainment on this island so we all make the best of any gathering.'

'Have you always lived here?' she asked.

'No, I came over here eleven years ago when I was twenty-two. I've been here ever since.'

'Do you go back often, home I mean?'

'Only when I have to,' he said.

She wanted to know more but he wasn't forthcoming with information. They were turning inland now across heathland towards the northern end of the island.

'What do you do for a living?' she asked.

'I survive. Work isn't everything. Most people worship it like a god. They spend most of their lives making as much money as they can then the rest worrying about what to do with it. I don't want that.'

'I agree, but unfortunately money is a necessity,' she said.

'Some, yes. Here on the island we are content just to make enough. I fish and grow my own food. There are plenty of trees for logs. I make a bit of cash from my boat, ferrying people to and from the island. It's enough.'

'Do you get many visitors on the island?'

'No, only people like your parents who love nature and come here to study it or just to relax. We don't cater for the average holiday-maker.'

She still couldn't reconcile this intelligent man with the simple life he seemed content to live.

He sensed her thoughts, 'I went to

agricultural college, got all the qualifications, but running an estate wasn't the life I wanted.'

'It seems an awful waste of your training but I think I understand,' she said, admiring his courage. 'What do your parents think?'

The road had become a narrow lane now and she could see grassy cliffs and the sea beyond.

'I live my life. They live theirs.' Again he was reticent.

'How about brothers and sisters, do you have any?'

'Yes, Alice is twenty-eight, very quiet and serious. Marie's the baby, only eighteen: lively, fun and always in trouble. I miss them both a lot.'

She wondered if Marie may be the woman in the photo, and maybe the child was part of the trouble. But the tension was there again, his jaw hardening and his eyes cold, so she felt she shouldn't ask any more questions.

The road ended abruptly and he pulled the car to a halt and jumped out.

'Come on,' he said, opening her door for her. He took both her hands and smiled, his eyes drawing her to him.

They scrambled down a grassy path and on to a ledge which led right round a precipice. As she stood looking out over the wide expanse of sea to the island of Canna in the distance, he stood behind her and she felt his arms slip round her waist. An excitement surged through her with the warmth of his body pressed against hers, his face close to her head, smelling clean and wholesome.

Involuntarily her hand moved to his arm and she felt the firm muscles and the soft hairs on his skin. As she turned her head he brushed his cheek close to hers and it seemed so comfortable and right.

Quickly she moved away slightly. He obviously wasn't interested in lasting relationships from what Hettie had said. She was only on the island for three weeks and then their paths would diverge again. This was just fun and she was beginning to feel alive again. It was what the holiday was all about and it was working.

His arm was still loosely round her waist as they turned and walked along the path. Cliffs rose high above them, grey and sheer, and on the gentler grassy slopes beneath them sheep grazed with their lambs.

'I can see why you like living here,' she said. 'It's so peaceful.'

There was a strange sound and they looked up to see two enormous eagles rise into the air and hover above the peaks.

'They're nesting up there,' he told her. 'We haven't seen them for several years, and now they're back again.'

Further round they came to a bay and watched seals playing in the warm current. Sitting on a rock they ate their simple picnic of chicken legs, fruit and white wine. Then she lay back against a grassy mound and let the sun beat down on her face and arms and listened to the sea breaking on rocks and the playful barking of the seals.

Robert propped himself on an elbow and looked down at her, smiling.

'I'm enjoying this,' she said, looking into his deep eyes.

'So am I.' Then something like pain touched his face, changing the smile. He sat upright and stared out far over the sea.

'What's wrong?' she asked.

He shrugged and looked back at her, the smile gone. 'Nothing, I was just thinking.'

What was he thinking? She put a hand gently on his arm and felt his muscles tense but he didn't respond and she was surprised at the slight stab of hurt she felt. They packed the picnic away and continued their walk but keeping their distance now, and Vanessa wondered what had happened to cause the change.

Robert so much wanted to take her hand as they walked along but something was stopping him. Why was he letting this happen? His emotions were all over the place. He couldn't keep away from her however hard he tried; yet he could not give himself to another woman, not ever.

Driving back in the car Robert suddenly slammed on the brakes and leaned out of the open window.

'The helicopter's landing on the Dunnin field. I wonder what's happened.' His voice was sharp with alarm. 'It usually means a medical emergency of some sort. The doctor can only do so much and there are no hospitals on the island.'

He put his foot down and they roared off at a frightening speed for the uneven road and she felt the chill of fear. Was it her father? Was it his heart again? How had they summoned help? A myriad of emotions swirled in her head.

When they arrived at the Dunnin field a group had gathered and Vanessa could see a stretcher being carefully handed on to the craft.

'It's Hettie,' Angus, the bearded man Vanessa recognised as the pipe-player at the ceilidh, told Robert. 'She took a bad turn in front of her class. One of the children ran for help. The doctor sent for the helicopter and she's in a pretty bad way, I think.'

A Shock For Vanessa

Vanessa's instant feeling of relief that it wasn't her father gave way to concern for the kind and friendly teacher who had taken her home after the ceilidh.

Robert went straight to the doctor and Vanessa watched their anxious conversation. Then the doors closed and the craft prepared to take off, the noisy blades making further talk impossible. They watched until it was a speck in the distance and then everyone crowded round Robert.

'The children will have to be sent home,' Maude's harsh voice informed him. 'Such a pity with the concert coming up. Goodness knows how long we'll be without a teacher. I don't suppose they'll send a replacement immediately.'

'The concert's a week next Saturday, isn't it?' Robert inquired. 'They're going to be disappointed.'

'Well my Morag can't take over. She's very good with the wee ones as you well know, but she's too busy in the tea shop now, especially with all these summer visitors arriving.'

Robert looked perplexed. 'I don't know what we can do. I'm no good at things like that myself. We'll have to send them home today, anyway. Who's with them now?'

'Fiona is. She had to close up the shop to see to them. Someone had better go and relieve her, and maybe take the wee ones home, but I've guests to cook for.'

'I could help,' Vanessa offered.

Robert looked round as if he'd forgotten she was there. 'I've worked with children before in theatre workshops. I'm not a teacher, but I could see them through the concert.'

His eyes lightened with relief. 'Of course you could!' Then to Maude, 'Vanessa's an actress, a gift from heaven.'

Maude looked decidedly disapproving, but Robert had made up his mind and grabbing Vanessa's hand, he pulled her rapidly back to the car and within minutes she found herself in the old school room where Fiona was trying to calm twelve frightened children.

'We need to contact the parents,' Fiona said. 'I could maybe take one or two home. But I really need to get back to the shop.'

'Look, I'll phone round,' Robert told her. 'Vanessa, here, can keep an eye on them while I find the numbers. We can cope between us. You get back.'

'Are you sure you don't mind?' Fiona asked her. Then she turned to Robert. 'What about the rehearsal for the concert tonight? I can't do it on my own. I was only helping Hettie. She's been doing the play with them and the singing and music. They're really not very good yet. They need a lot of practice. We were going to rehearse every evening until the concert. I'll never be able to get it all together without her.'

Robert put his arm round Vanessa's shoulders. 'This is our saviour. Vanessa's an actress. She's volunteered to help out.' He turned to Vanessa. 'Can you be there about five tonight at the Ceilidh Hall and help Fiona. I'm sure that together you can pull it off.'

'Would you do that, Vanessa? The children could go ahead with their concert then and it would help cheer them up. They're very worried about their teacher.'

'Yes, of course,' Vanessa reassured her. Fiona gave her a grateful smile and rushed off.

Robert disappeared in search of phone numbers and she was left in temporary charge of the children while he contacted their parents to come and take them home. She could hear him already talking to one of them just outside the door.

Twelve pairs of eyes stared at her. 'Hello, I'm Vanessa and I'm going to look after you for a few minutes. Will you tell me your names? They answered politely but nothing more. They looked so miserable and she wondered what she could do to keep them occupied until they were taken home.

There was an assortment of musical instruments piled in the corner behind an old upright piano.

'Can you let me hear you sing?' she asked them.

The twelve pairs of eyes still stared silently. She went to the piano and lifted the lid, but the old nursery songs she'd learnt as a child produced no response either.

'Can any of you play these instruments?' she tried. Nobody moved.

For half-an-hour she persevered, wondering when the parents would begin to arrive, but there didn't seem to be any sign of them and Robert had disappeared as well, telling her he was going to try to locate them in the fields.

Despondently she sat down on the desk chair. Looking up she noticed the smallest girl drag a chubby hand across her face to wipe away a tear. An older boy put his arm comfortingly round her and seeing Vanessa watch, said, 'Emma's upset about Mrs McPhearson, Miss.'

Vanessa groaned at her own stupidity in expecting the children to sing and play when they were upset. She rose slowly from the desk. 'Yes, of course, Jamie, you all are. But you mustn't worry. Mrs McPhearson's not very well so she's going to hospital.'

'Will she get better?' Jamie asked.

'She's in very good hands, Jamie, and we'll soon know how she's getting on,' Vanessa reassured him.

'When will she come back?' Hannah asked.

'I'm sure she'll be back here in no time. Now, how about a card? Would you all like to make Mrs McPhearson a Get Well card to cheer her up?'

'Can we put glitter on it?'

'Can I cut it out? Mrs McPhearson always lets me cut out 'cos she says I'm sensible with scissors.'

'No, she doesn't. She lets all of us have a turn.'

Within minutes they had found scissors and glue and were busy pasting and painting round the big table producing a large card, each contributing and helping the younger ones.

She soon became immersed in the activity and was surprised when Fiona appeared again, this time with Angus. One or two of the other parents arrived and eventually all the children had been taken home.

As the last child left the room a pair of large round eyes looked up at her. 'I like you; will you come again tomorrow?'

'No, Emma, you will have another teacher until Mrs McPhearson gets better, but I'll be at your rehearsal tonight to help Fiona, so I'll see you then.'

When she went along to the hall for the rehearsal Fiona was already there with some of the mums and most of the children. They soon had them on stage going through the play. Vanessa groaned inwardly. They knew their lines but the whole thing was a disaster. Some shouted, others mumbled and none of them put any feeling into it. She would have her work cut out here.

* * *

By Friday the replacement teacher had still not arrived but the concert preparations were well under way and Vanessa was amazed at how much the children had improved. They were a talented little group and responded well to her encouragement in modifying and adding to the performance they had been working on with Hettie.

It had been a long session and they were tired. Fiona and some of the other mums were in the back room sorting out the costumes before taking their children home. She was tidying away the instruments when Hannah tugged at her sleeve.

'I can't wait for the concert,' she said excitedly. 'I've got a really important part, haven't I?'

'No, you haven't,' Jamie piped up. 'I'm the Gingerbread Man. That's the most important part of all.'

'Now stop all this,' Vanessa chided. 'I think you've all done really well. How would you like a story?'

'Will you make one up like yesterday?' Emma asked.

'Will you act it as well? Will you be a fire-eating dragon again?' Jamie pleaded.

'You'll just have to wait and see what the story's about, won't you? Now sit down in a circle on the floor and be very quiet.'

There was complete silence as she made up her story, their faces upturned in adoration. One minute she was a giant toad leaping around the floor and then, after a significant pause, she donned a hat and cape and dramatically changed into a handsome prince, and the children clapped and squealed in delight.

Suddenly all eyes turned to the door where Robert stood grinning at her. He must have entered amidst the uproar

58

and she had not heard him.

She felt embarrassed and irritated that he should sneak up on her like that. With the children she could relax and escape into a fairytale world because they accepted it, just as on stage the audience was prepared to suspend disbelief, but in front of Robert she just felt foolish.

'Do you want a lift home?' Fiona asked her when the other children had been taken by their parents.

'No, thanks Fiona, I need to run through some of the music before I go.'

'I'm sure Robert, here, will see you home safely.' Fiona smiled at her.

Vanessa sighed. 'I'm sure he will.'

'Vanessa, why are you so angry with me?' he asked when they were alone, his face changing to show concern.

'You shouldn't creep up on me like that. You asked me to help out. I'm doing my best. I'm an actress, not a teacher. I'm getting them ready for the concert. When they get tired I entertain them. Is there anything wrong with that?'

He put up his hands in mock defence.

'I'm not criticising. In fact just the opposite. I'm full of admiration for the way you're coping. And before you bite my head off again, I didn't sneak in, I came to ask you to have dinner with me.'

His eyes sparkled and an affectionate smile played on his mouth. It was impossible to be annoyed with him for long.

She gave a resigned smile. 'That would be lovely.'

'Good, we'll tidy up here then I'll drive you back to my cottage. We can relax there without being disturbed.'

An uncomfortable feeling crept over her but she brushed it aside.

★ ★ ★

Fisherman's Cottage was high on the cliffs at the south of the island, with the road petering out to a narrow track long before it was reached.

'It's so isolated,' she commented as his old car pulled up at the side.

'I like it that way,' he smiled and helped her out. 'If you scream here nobody will hear you.'

She registered instant alarm but his smiling eyes soon set her fears to rest.

It was tiny but cosy. Whitewashed walls and thatch outside, deep wooden beams and a brick fireplace inside. Within minutes she was sitting by a crackling log fire with a glass in her hand.

Smelling that it was whisky in her glass, she grimaced and handed it back.

'It's a fine matured malt,' he assured her raising his own glass. 'Just a tot warms the soul and mellows the heart.'

She took a sip and liked the warm glow it produced.

'It's not much of a holiday for you, coping with all those children,' he called from the kitchen.

The same thing had occurred to her and yet strangely she had found it more therapeutic than sitting around moping.

At least she hadn't had time to think about Greg.

'That cooking smells lovely,' she called to him happily lulled by the crackle of burning logs and the sound of Robert preparing their meal in the kitchen.

'It's lamb, reared here on the island. You haven't tasted anything until you've tried this,' he called back.

They sat at an old oak table by a window overlooking the bay and Vanessa savoured every mouthful. They spoke little, just content to be together watching the waves gently wash up on the shingle and gulls circling the cliffs.

'That was delicious,' she said eventually, pushing her chair back and beginning to clear the plates away, but Robert firmly took her by the shoulders and marched her to the fireside. 'No more work for you today, my girl.'

Somehow his arms slid round her and she was facing him. His face was heavy with passion and their lips touched. It was the lightest of touches and then his hands went up into her hair and brought her to him and he kissed her with great longing.

Eventually he let her go but still gazed at her with intensity. 'You're so lovely,' he murmured. Every nerve in her body was responding to his touch, his look, his closeness.

Then he took her hand. 'Come on, let's go outside and watch the sunset over the sea.'

'It's so still out there,' she said almost to herself.

'Not always,' he replied. 'It can be cruel and menacing.' He let her hand drop and walked ahead of her to the fence and, gripping at a wooden post, stared out, a sudden anger taking hold of him. Then he strode back to her, his jaw set and eyes hard.

She followed him back inside, not knowing what had caused the change but sure that something was wrong.

He clattered around in the kitchen, made coffee, put logs on the fire and still his anger smouldered.

'What's the matter, Robbie?' she asked.

He swung round on her. 'Don't call me that,' he snapped.

She was shocked. 'I'm sorry, but Robert sounds so formal.'

'It's my name and I like it that way,' he said.

She was hurt and confused. Tiredness made her more touchy and tears threatened.

'I think perhaps I'd better go,' she said shakily.

He struggled for control and then turned to her and took her hands. It was too much and the tears began to pour down her face. He pulled her to him and, rocking her gently in his arms, spoke softly. 'I'm sorry, Vanessa. I shouldn't have snapped like that. I can't explain, but hearing you call me that name — someone else used to use it, someone special. Nobody else has ever called me that.'

A vision of the photograph of the woman and child she had seen in his cabin on the boat came before her eyes and she choked back a large sob in her throat. 'I'm sorry. Whatever I've done to upset you, I'm sorry, but I really would like to go home. I'm very tired.'

His arms still held her firmly and his hand stroked her hair.

'Please, will you take me home now?'

He looked down at her but didn't argue, then got her jacket and took her out to the car.

When he got back to his cottage Robert fell into a chair feeling totally dejected. What right had he to do this to her? He was upsetting and hurting her all the time, all because of his own weakness and inadequacy. He must keep away from her, not see her again. She didn't understand and he couldn't explain. How would any woman understand what was going on in his head? He didn't want to share it with anyone anyway.

★　★　★

Vanessa woke early next morning quite determined to enjoy the rest of her stay and to forget all about Robert.

'You seem very cheerful this morning,' Audrey said.

'Yes, I am. What are you two doing today? Can I join you?'

Audrey was surprised and delighted. 'Yes, of course. Dad wants to go round to the west coast and study the rock pools.'

'Oh, good, I can go snorkelling. Did you bring the wetsuit?'

'Yes, I'll go and find it.'

'How will we get there?' Vanessa asked.

'We've hired a motorboat. Angus will take us down to the jetty then we'll take it from there.'

'Sounds fun. Do I get to steer?'

Audrey laughed. 'You'll have to sort that out with your father. Now you will need some sensible clothes. Those jeans will do but not the shoes.'

'Here we go again. Do you have any I can borrow?'

'It's a good job we take the same size. You can have these,' Audrey said, producing a pair of canvas sailing shoes.

★　★　★

The rock pools were magic, the warm Gulf Stream encouraging a wealth of species. Geoff set to work immediately with a net delving into unknown depths to see what he could trawl while her mother sat with binoculars, watching the birds along the cliffs and on the shore below.

Vanessa got into the wetsuit and cringed as the icy water crept between the rubber and her skin.

'It's freezing, Mum!' She groaned.

Audrey laughed. 'Of course it is. Once the water's crept up and warmed, you'll be fine.'

The snorkel in place, she ducked under and was quickly lost in the magnificence of shape and colour in the clear water. Giant towering corals and wavy ferns intermingled to give a fairytale land with a life of its own.

'Soup's poured out,' her mother called and she couldn't believe she'd been in the cold water for over half-an-hour.

Cupping the hot soup in her hands she crouched above a tiny rock pool and marvelled at the wonderful shades of mauve, grey, green and hints of red in it, big blobby sea anemones and the sudden dart of a silver fish.

'Just look at the sea anemone, Vanessa, and see what I've got here, a hermit crab. You just don't get this variety of wildlife elsewhere in the country.'

'I'm sure you do, Dad,' Vanessa laughed. Her father's fascination with small creatures had always amused her.

The afternoon passed peacefully as she lay dozing in the sun and watching cotton wool clouds drift by.

'Are we ready to make a move, girls?' Geoff asked, bringing her back from her daydreaming.

'Do we have to?' Vanessa moaned. 'I

could stay here all day.'

'We almost have, but I think it's time we got back now. Dad's looking a bit tired. I'll just pack everything up,' Audrey said.

'OK, just give me five minutes to get ready.'

They drifted along the coast with the gentle lap of water and sea birds swooping and diving all around them.

'Do you want to take over now, Dad?' Vanessa asked as they approached the jetty, and she handed the wheel to her father.

'Well, if you insist, but you can take her alongside just as easily as me.'

'You're very kind, but we all know you're the expert. I'd rather you did the final manoeuvre. I don't want to take the paint off.'

Then her heart stopped. Robert was standing on the quay outside the little teashop in deep conversation with a pretty dark-haired woman of about her own age. She felt the blood drain from her face and her legs began to tremble.

She gripped the rail in an effort to keep upright but never took her eyes off the pair. The woman looked her way and smiled.

'Are you all right, Vanessa?' her mother asked. 'You've gone very pale.'

'Yes, Mum, I just feel a bit light headed.'

'Sit down, dear. Maybe you overdid the snorkelling.'

'I'm fine, Mum.' Vanessa said. 'Please, don't fuss.'

She sat down as her father brought the craft alongside, her mother looking concerned. Her heart was pounding in her chest and she couldn't stop shaking.

It was the face in the photo. The woman Robert was talking to was the woman in the photo that Robert had hanging over his bed in his boat, the woman who had haunted her dreams over the past week.

When Robert saw them unloading the boat he smiled and waved in a casual manner and then, turning his back, walked inside with the woman.

She felt her resolve slipping away. She

shouldn't care, but she did care. She cared a lot. Now it all made sense. She had thought he was different. Greg, now Robert. She would never trust a man again. All you ended up with was a broken heart. With enormous will power she calmed her nerves and brought her trembling limbs under control.

'How about a cup of tea?' Geoff asked when they were half way up the jetty.

'Yes, now that's a good idea,' Audrey said, giving Vanessa a worried look. 'A sit down and a cup of tea will make you feel better.'

Vanessa's mind was not working fast enough to avoid being ushered into the pleasant, airy room with chintz curtains and red checked tablecloths. When Robert saw them come in he finished his conversation with the woman and came over to them.

'And did you find anything interesting?' he asked Geoff.

'There's a great variety of sea life in those rock pools,' her father said. 'And Vanessa enjoyed looking around under

71

the water. Too cold for me, I'm afraid, after my heart attack. Have to look after myself now.'

'Quite right, too,' Robert said.

'And how about you, Mrs Sanderson? Did you see the eagles?'

'No, but the seals were lovely.'

'Yes, we are very lucky here with our wildlife. Nothing much to disturb it, you see.'

'I hope you can keep it that way. Once the tourist trade builds up it may change,' Audrey said.

'Oh, no, I don't think that will be a problem,' Robert said. 'Only people like yourselves will come here. Nothing to attract the average holiday maker.'

Vanessa tried not to look at Robert but looked at the pictures on the walls.

'Enjoy your tea, then,' Robert smiled. 'Morag, here, makes very good cakes. You should indulge yourselves.'

'We will,' Audrey assured him.

Morag served them in a cheerful and friendly manner.

'We have nine more people arriving

this afternoon. Robert is bringing them in the boat,' Morag said.

'Wherever will they stay?' Audrey asked.

'They're staying in the guesthouse over at Louver with my mother. They're a party of geologists come to study the island's rock formation.'

So Maude ran a guesthouse and this was her daughter. It explained why Maude didn't approve of her.

'Does Robert ferry all the visitors to and from the island?' her mother asked.

Morag smiled. 'Och, he does most things round here.'

'Don't Let Him Get
To You, Vanessa'

By Tuesday Vanessa was getting anxious. Saturday's performance was coming along well due to the enthusiasm of the children, but nobody had informed her of any plans for rehearsals or what facilities there would be for the children to change or how to get stage props and instruments to the hall.

'Robert sees to all that,' Fiona assured her when she popped into the shop for some milk for breakfast.

'Yes, but Robert hasn't shown his face since last Friday.'

Fiona was a little taken aback. 'I'm sure he's organised everything just fine. He never lets us down.'

'But where is he?' Vanessa asked impatiently.

'Vanessa, please don't worry. I'm sure

he will have arranged things with Maude. And Angus will know what is to be done. My father-in-law is indispensable at times like this.'

'I didn't know Angus was your father-in-law,' Vanessa said, surprised.

'We're pretty well all related on this island. He does help me a lot when my Duncan's away on the mainland delivering his pottery, looks after the shop while I go out and he's very close to young Jamie. Anyway don't you fret, all will work out just fine, you'll see.'

'I'm sorry, Fiona. I didn't mean to get at you.'

Fiona put an arm round her shoulder. 'Are you a wee bit sweet on our Robert?'

Vanessa pulled away. 'No, Fiona, you can't think that.'

'Well, you wouldn't be the first. All the girls fall in love with him as soon as they see him. But they never get anywhere. Don't let him get to you, Vanessa.'

'Fiona, I am not interested in Robert,

other than getting his co-operation with this concert. I just want it to go smoothly for the children's sake.'

'It'll go just fine,' Fiona said.

Vanessa wanted to be sure so decided to find Robert and ask him directly, so she told her parents she would join them later on the beach and set off to walk to his cottage. She had a note in her pocket to pop through his letterbox in case he was out.

The walk was invigorating, through grassy meadows where sheep grazed with their lambs. The yellow blaze of wild iris by the stream and the gentle sound of water running beside the path all added their magic and a skylark rose high with its distinctive song, lifting her spirits.

The cottage door was open and her stomach gave a lurch in anticipation of confronting him. She had been half hoping, and in fact expecting, that he would not be there.

The sound of radio music drowned her knock so in desperation she eventually walked in.

The living room was a shambles of upturned furniture, and amongst the chaos Maude was attacking the carpet with a stiff brush. She looked up and quickly straightened her apron and then reached for the radio to turn off the music.

'I'm sorry, Miss Sanderson, I didn't hear you coming. Did you want to speak with me?'

'I was wondering if Robert was here,' she said lamely, her legs only just supporting her.

'Well, no, he's gone away back to the mainland and I couldn't tell you when he'll be back. Maybe not for a week or more. Was there something you needed?'

Vanessa swallowed. 'It was just about the concert on Saturday.'

'Yes, well I do have a message about that. He says Angus will see to the instruments and my Morag's doing the refreshments. You'll be looking after the children and the parents will help set it up.'

'Well, I must say he's very good at organising people in his absence,' she said bitterly.

'He's a fine young man. Best thing that ever happened to this island.' Maude gave her a distrusting look and continued her onslaught on the carpet, making further conversation impossible.

Coughing from the rising dust and feeling decidedly ill-used, Vanessa made her way back across the fields. Robert McKenzie would not get away with this.

★ ★ ★

Greg's letter arrived on Friday.

My Dear Vanessa,

She has gone. Mandy is no more, dismissed from my life forever. You are the one, the only one. Please, please, please return to the fold. We miss you. I miss you. We need you. The Cheltern Players cannot survive without you. The next production will be the best.

We are to attempt The Tempest. The height of my aspirations! And I want you to produce it. I give you a free hand, I promise. I shall play Prospero. Please, forgive me. How can I live without you?

'What's the matter, dear?' Audrey had come into the room with two cups of tea. She put one on the small table by Vanessa's chair then perched on the edge of the chair opposite.

'It's from Greg.' Vanessa let the letter fall on to her lap. 'He wants me back.'

'Is that what you want?'

'I don't know, Mum. I do miss him.'

'But he did treat you badly. Do be careful. If he can do that sort of thing once, he could always do it again.'

Vanessa sighed. 'Yes, I know, and he has done it before, several times. But we had some good times and I still care about him. If only I thought I could trust him.'

'I don't think you can.'

'He wants me to produce their new play. It's what I've wanted for a long

79

time and it would be a good place to start. But I will think carefully about it, don't worry, Mum.'

Her mother gave her a reassuring smile and left her to her thoughts.

She made several attempts at a reply but they sounded inadequate, so she finally decided that after what he had done he didn't deserve a reply, so she ripped his letter up, together with her efforts at a reply, and dropped them into the bin.

★　★　★

Preparations for the concert began early on Saturday morning. Fiona worked alongside Vanessa sorting out the costumes and stage props and Vanessa wondered how she could have coped without her.

Maude was to sing, so practised her mystical ballads with the pianist. Then the ceilidh band arrived with their instruments.

Vanessa tried to rehearse with the children in the hall, but found the various activities were distracting.

Then Maude complained, 'How am I to sing my songs with the children making all that noise?'

'Don't fuss, Mother,' Morag told her. 'Vanessa has to sort them out. And you know your songs so well; I don't know why you bother to rehearse. You sing the same ones every year.'

Maude bridled at this. 'And that is due to respect. People here like the old songs and they like things the way they've always been, no changing all the time.

'I don't believe all these visitors with their fancy ideas do the island any good at all.' She gave Vanessa a significant look.

Morag smiled. 'Our business wouldn't do too well if they stayed away. Who'd stay at our guesthouse or visit my teashop?' She caught Vanessa's eye and winked. 'And who do you think would have got our wee bairns organised to perform tonight?'

Maude gave Vanessa a withering look

and returned to her trilling melodies.

'Don't take any notice of Mother,' Morag said as she passed Vanessa. 'She thinks she's a bit of a virtuoso when it comes to singing, and the concert is her chance to shine. You carry on with your arrangements.'

Vanessa sighed. She could have really taken to Morag. She was sweet and friendly. But she felt awkward in her presence and mad at Robert for his deception.

As Maude chided the pianist and flicked her music irritably, Vanessa felt her already fragile ego sinking. There was activity all round her of which she had no part. She was, as Maude had implied, an outsider who should be scrambling up the mountains or pitting her skills against the elements in a sailing dinghy. Anything but organising the island's children in the most important event on the island's calendar and attracting the attention, if unintentionally, of their only eligible bachelor.

A child's hand tugged at her sleeve bringing her back to the task in hand. 'Vanessa, my costume is torn.'

'Don't fuss, Hannah, I'll see to it in a minute.'

'Jamie pulled it, Vanessa. He did it on purpose.'

'All right, I've said I'll fix it. Now go and put those flowers on the stage as I told you to.'

Hannah sniffed but went obediently to do her job.

'I'm going out for a while,' she told Fiona.

'Are you all right, Vanessa?' Fiona gave her a worried look.

'I have a headache and I need some fresh air.'

'You go and relax, there's nothing more to do here just now. You will be back later, won't you?'

'Fiona, I won't let you down, I promise.'

Fiona gave her a relieved smile. 'I know you won't.'

At six o'clock Vanessa walked back

into the hall and began her final check on the props and costumes.

When all was ready and the children were assembled to take their place on stage to sing their first medley of songs Fiona rushed up to Vanessa.

'Vanessa, Jamie has just been sick and he's as white as a ghost. It's probably just nerves but I'm sure he won't be able to do a thing.'

'Oh, no, poor Jamie.'

'What will we do?' Fiona was distraught. 'We have no Gingerbread Man now.'

'No understudies either,' Vanessa mused.

'No, none. Oh, Vanessa what can we do? The whole play will be ruined. The children will be so upset. I'm sure Jamie can't do it. He's taken really badly.'

Fiona looked as if she was about to burst into tears so Vanessa put an arm round her shoulder to comfort her.

'Don't look so glum. Let's see if Jamie recovers. We have until after the interval before he's due on stage.'

The audience assembled, a noisy

disorganised crowd, exchanging news and chattering happily.

The musicians began to play and the voices silenced. The children marched on to the stage under Fiona's directions. They sang loud and clear and everyone applauded enthusiastically. Maude produced many watery eyes with her Celtic folk songs. The doctor recited some amusing monologues and then it was time for tea and cakes.

Vanessa tried her best to revive Jamie and persuade him that if he just put the costume on he'd be fine and really enjoy the performance. But all efforts of bribery and persuasion left Jamie listless and pale with no desire to do anything other than lie under a blanket and moan.

'Who'll be the Gingerbread Man?' Emma asked timidly.

Hannah nudged her. 'Don't ask silly questions. We won't have one.'

'But we can't do the play without the Gingerbread Man.'

Emma began to sob and pleading eyes turned on Vanessa until she knew her fate was sealed. Well, it wasn't the greatest challenge she'd come up against in her career.

'Right, I'll do it. Now all of you stop fussing and get ready to go on.'

Again the children stared at her, and so did Fiona and Maude and the entire band. She dived into the costume box to find something vaguely gingerbread coloured that would fit her and came out with a hairy, brown bear outfit that she thought she could adapt.

Fiona explained to the audience what had happened and Vanessa strolled on to the stage as the Gingerbread Man to an uproar of cheering and clapping.

The performance was an outstanding success. The children loved it. The audience loved it and laughed and clapped until their hands hurt and their sides ached. She had not only carried the part off well but also carried the children along with her. Everyone was with her and she knew that the only thing these generous people wanted was a good time.

When she finally stood, hot and breathless, to take the final applause, surrounded by all the children, the audience was on its feet, so was the band and the whole place was in uproar.

Then she saw him at the back of the hall leaning against the doors grinning and shaking his head in disbelief. Robert had caught her making a fool of herself again.

Suddenly she felt very tired and just wanted to go home. She changed the children, handed them over to their parents, accepted their praise and thanks and then tidied away the costumes.

By this time everyone had dispersed and she found herself alone in the back section of the old hall, wishing that she hadn't insisted her parents went on back to the cottage without her. Company on the walk home would have been welcome.

She was just about to turn off the gaslights and leave when she heard footsteps echoing on the wooden boards and Robert appeared round the door.

Despite her tiredness a wave of excitement passed through her at the sight of his tall figure.

'I'll see you home,' he said.

'There's no need.' She was determined not to give in to him.

He stood in front of her, serious now. Then he sighed.

She pushed past him into the night. 'I'll leave you to close the door, Robert,' and she began to stride off.

He grabbed her arm and spun her round to face him. 'Vanessa, will you tell me why you're mad at me?'

She faced him squarely and his eyes were serious now, deep and penetrating, almost, but not quite weakening her resolve.

'I am not mad at you but I have had enough of children and concerts and running around organising things that are no concern of mine while you go swanning off to goodness knows where.' She was flushed and out of breath and, to her great discomfort, he was grinning at her.

'That's the best bit of play acting I've seen you do yet. The Gingerbread Man was very convincing, but this is even better.'

'What do you mean?' she barked at him.

'I mean that everything you've just said is complete fabrication. Firstly, you are mad at me, secondly you're a natural with children and you've enjoyed every minute of it, and thirdly you're not the type to lounge around on holiday doing nothing so you wouldn't enjoy it anyway.'

'Just give me the chance,' she shouted and stormed off along the road, her heel twisting awkwardly on a stone.

She could feel him watching her in the moonlight, his dark eyes penetrating her back. She tried not to limp although her ankle hurt, and she tried not to believe that what he had said was true. It was disconcerting to know he could read her so easily.

It was over a mile of rough road back to her cottage and in flimsy shoes and with a twisted ankle every step was painful. The day's activity had taken its toll and she longed for the comfort and oblivion of bed. Tears were welling already and she sniffed to keep them at bay, trying desperately to think positively, keep your mind on the week ahead and her plans to leave the island to begin a new future and a new career.

She had finally written to Greg and told him plainly that their relationship was over. It had been a difficult decision to make and even as she had written the letter she had longed for his arms around her and the happiness they had shared.

She was so lost in thought that the sound of a car drawing up beside her made her turn in shock. It was only when Robert stood before her, his tall figure framed in the moonlight, that she was again conscious of her painful ankle and the tears that were streaming down her face.

He took one look at her and, before she could resist, he had circled her in his strong arms. At first she drew back but his strength soon overcame her and she allowed herself to be held without resistance, momentarily grateful for the security and warmth he offered, and they remained so for endless moments.

'Vanessa, don't push me away from you,' he whispered and she could sense the urgency in his voice. 'You're tired and upset. I know I've treated you badly and I'm sorry. Now I'm going to take you home.'

He guided her round to the side of the car, kissed her wet cheek, and then gently helped her in.

By the time they reached Dove Cottage her tears had dried and she could almost manage a smile. He stopped the engine and reaching over to the back seat, produced a plastic carrier bag which he gave to her. She stared at it and then at him.

'Go on, open it,' he said.

She felt in the bag and pulled out something silky in a rich dark colour which she could not quite distinguish in the moonlight.

'It's a dress,' he said. 'I hope I got the right size.'

She felt the silky softness of it and looked up at him again unable to believe what she was seeing.

'You needn't have done this,' she said huskily. 'I have enjoyed working with the children, you were right about that. I didn't expect a thank you present.'

'That's not what it is,' he said. 'I just saw it and thought of you so I bought it.'

'Oh!' The tears were threatening again so she had to think fast to lighten the mood. 'I didn't think you approved of clothes like this. You're always telling me I should wear something sensible.'

He moved closer to her and his arm slid round her shoulders, his cheek close to hers.

'You should when we're trekking round the island or picnicking on the beach. But it would be a shame for such a beautiful woman not to dress in beautiful clothes for the right occasion.'

His face was very close, his voice seductively low. 'Tomorrow, Janice and Steven are having a party. I'm picking you all up at eight, everyone's invited.' His mouth closed over hers, and for a moment all thought of Morag was gone.

Then she pulled away and jumped out of the car slamming the door behind her.

Standing in the moonlight in front of the cottage she lifted the dress to her face, feeling its silky softness, then quickly pulled it away again so that the tears welling up in her eyes would not damage the beautiful fabric. If only Robert was taking her to the party instead of just giving them all a lift. Her heart was so full she felt it must burst with love and sadness.

Robert felt a warm glow as he drove away. She would look spectacular in the dress and tomorrow he would take her to the party and they would be close again. If only he could give his heart to her. But her's rested elsewhere and soon she would be gone to pursue her career and he would remain here with his guilt and sorrow.

An Unexpected Visitor Arrives

'Well, you look a treat, my girl,' Geoff said, looking at Vanessa with pride. 'Audrey, doesn't she look lovely?'

They both stood admiring her in her new red dress.

'That really is your colour, dear, with your dark hair and pale skin,' her mother said. 'It's so nice of Robert to pick us up. It's eight o'clock now so he should be here any minute.'

'I think his car has just pulled up,' Geoff announced. 'Are we all ready?'

Feeling light and happy Vanessa opened the door when she heard his knock and beamed at him.

'Wow!' was all he could manage.

The party was in full swing when they arrived. It was of special interest to most of the islanders because Steven and Janice Bright had only recently settled on the island, having taken on one of the larger houses with the intention of turning it into a small hotel. This was their first party and everyone was invited and came.

As it was such a warm evening the food had been set out in the garden and a barbecue was under way. Vanessa was whisked off by Janice and introduced to as many people as Janice could remember the names of. Then Steven appeared hot from the barbecue and offered her a smoky hand.

Fiona came over and complemented her on the concert and how well she had carried it off.

'You all seem to enjoy life here,' Vanessa commented.

'Och, I'd never get my Duncan away from this island, not in a million years. He hates going back to the mainland but he has some good outlets for the pottery he makes. Sometimes I think it would be nice to live nearer to civilisation but then I enjoy running the shop and it's a good life for wee Jamie while he's young. But when he goes to secondary school we shall miss him and I don't know how Duncan will feel then. He's very close to the bairn.'

She saw the doctor and went over to ask him about Hettie. He was a portly man with a shock of white hair and a smiling face.

'She's doing just fine, now. We can expect her back on the island in a week or two,' he told her.

'The children will be pleased,' she said.

'She'll not be back at school for a while. I did hear they were sending someone over but the poor lady has gone down with the flu, so I expect we'll be without a teacher for a while longer.'

'But what about the children?'

'I expect Robert will be seeing to it,' he said.

'But surely it isn't his responsibility.'

He gave her a strange questioning look then turned away to re-light his pipe.

'He does seem to concern himself

with everything that goes on here,' she persisted.

He inhaled deeply then turned to her again. 'Aye, he's a good man. We're all very fond of our Robert.'

Vanessa groaned inwardly. What was it about this man that everyone fell at his feet?

Then she found herself propelled over to the barbecue and a plate put in her hand. Steven loaded it with chicken and kebabs before she had a chance to refuse and then she saw Robert standing in a far corner of the garden talking to Morag, her small figure looking up at him.

She turned her back on them and went over to join Janice.

'I really admire your enthusiasm,' Vanessa said as they stood in the dilapidated kitchen. 'I hear you've done it before on one of the other islands. How wonderful to turn something like this into a living thing again.'

'It will only be small, but the house has such character. It is run down but I think we can make it very comfortable,' she told her. 'We are a little inhibited this time, not being able to buy the property. All the profits from the business of course will come to us and the rent is modest, but it does put one off spending too much on renovations.'

'You mean all your efforts will put the landlord's property in order without it costing him a penny.'

'I'm afraid so. The island is part of a big estate and the landlord owns all the property.'

'So nobody can buy a house here?'

'That's about it.'

'I think that's terrible,' Vanessa said.

A deep voice behind her butted in. 'It is.'

She turned and saw Robert standing behind her.

'I wondered where you were, but I see you are being taken good care of,' he said.

'Perhaps you'd like to show Vanessa round, Robert,' Janice said, then turning to Vanessa, 'It's in much better condition in parts.'

Vanessa couldn't think of any way out of this without seeming rude so she let Robert take her hand and guide her through the rather dilapidated rooms.

'I think it's wrong that one man should own a whole island, the homes of people who have lived here all their lives, make rules about a place and people he doesn't even know.'

Robert was serious. 'I agree and I'm doing my best to change it.'

She looked at him with raised eyebrows. 'You are?'

'Don't look so surprised. I thought you would approve.'

'Well, yes, of course. But how are you going to do it? I mean if someone owns the land you can't just wade in and take it away from them. And you can't change the law single handed.'

'I don't intend to. When the time is right I shall make my move.'

So that was it. It explained why he was so secretive, why he was away on the mainland so often, why he interested himself in everything that went on round the island and why he was so well respected. But what exactly was he up to. A sudden uneasiness made her shudder.

As they went into the library his arm slipped round her as he pointed to a wall of leather bound volumes.

'Don't,' she snapped and wriggled away.

He stood back and looked at her, a hurt surprised look.

Something about his look demanded an explanation and he felt the need to get things straight between them.

'What about Morag?' she said defensively.

'Morag, why should she care?'

Then his expression changed. 'Vanessa, you don't think that Morag — ' he stopped and came round in front of her, his face serious. 'Vanessa, I have a deep affection for Morag but it is not romantic. I have no romantic attachments; otherwise I would not be paying attention to you. I'm not that sort of man, I can assure you.'

His eyes held hers with such intensity she felt forced to believe him, wanted to believe him, and yet she wasn't convinced.

'But the photo. The one in your cabin on the boat. I saw it the day you brought us here.'

He sighed. 'The photo. Yes, I see now. That photo isn't of Morag.'

'But it looks like her with a child.'

Then he looked away and his voice was almost inaudible. 'It was her sister. And the child . . . ' His voice trailed away. He was struggling with his emotions. Then he turned to her with pain-filled eyes. 'Vanessa, I can't explain now. Please, let's go back to the party.'

Robert was very quiet for the rest of the evening and Vanessa couldn't take her mind off what he had said. Morag watched them closely and Vanessa felt vaguely uncomfortable under her scrutiny, so was not disappointed when Robert suggested they leave.

'I don't want to drag you away but I do have to make a call on the new arrivals at The Hole. They should be there now and I want to make sure they have everything they need,' he explained.

'You really do take care of everything, don't you?' she said.

He smiled, seeming to have recovered completely now from their conversation earlier. 'I should have gone over for them on the boat but I wanted to bring you to this party. You should be flattered, you know. I usually take my boatman duties very seriously but this party was left to the mercy of the ferry.'

'How about Mum and Dad?' Vanessa asked.

'They've gone with the doctor. He wanted your dad to try some of his collection of single malt whiskies. Bit of a connoisseur, our doc. They'll be fine. He'll see them home later.'

Vanessa felt a little uneasy at this arrangement but accepted that she couldn't do much about it and just hoped the doctor was capable of taking her parents home after the whisky tasting session.

They said their farewells and slipped away from the party and Vanessa was happy to be alone with Robert in his comfortable old car.

'We'll pop into The Hole and make sure all is well then I'll take you back to my place for a drink. We can talk quietly there.'

The Hole was a large wooden structure in the hillside with a corrugated tin roof, practical but not as picturesque as the cottages.

'I think it's important to build up the tourist industry on the island but without destroying its character. It's a fine lead to tread. But it's the only hope for the people. Too many have left already,' he told her.

She couldn't help thinking he was assuming an awful lot of responsibility, then it struck her that maybe he had wheedled his way into a position of trust in order to further his own ends.

Robert jumped out of the car and

knocked loudly on the door. Gaslights glowed dimly from every room showing evidence of people settling in and putting things away. When the door opened she shot bolt upright.

Ken Price, the best actor the Cheltern had ever seen, had stood straight and stocky, filling the door. Appearing behind him she saw Denise, their wardrobe mistress and Felicity who had worked so hard to make their last play a success. Here were her friends and a sudden overpowering homesickness came over her. She leapt out of the car and round to the door.

Ken put his arm around her shoulders and Felicity hugged her. 'Darling, how are you? Shut away up here all on your own. We felt we must come and rescue you.'

Vanessa pulled away trying to make sense of it all and was aware of Robert standing quietly aside watching her. She turned to speak to him, and then from a back room, appeared a tall blond figure and her heart did a somersault.

There was a complete and deadly silence as their eyes met, her legs went weak and a sense of unreality took over.

He didn't speak for a moment and then a smile transformed his face and lit up his deep blue eyes. 'Hello, darling, you're looking as beautiful as ever. I'm glad the Highlands of Scotland haven't destroyed your style.'

She was unaware of anyone else in the room as the whole trauma flooded back. His eyes still had the power to hold her, his astounding good looks to melt her resolve.

'I wrote to you,' she stammered.

'Jolly good. I shall look forward to reading your epistle when I return to the land of the living. In the meantime I intend to have the real thing, and take it back with me,' he grinned.

'No, that's not possible,' she said backing away and trying to tear her eyes from him. 'I'm moving on, not back.'

Felicity began fussing. 'It will be all right, Vanessa. Mandy West has left now. She caused a lot of trouble for all of us. You've just got to come back with us. Greg says you can produce our next play which is what you've always wanted.'

'I won't interfere,' Greg promised, hands spread in front of him.

The place was a shambles of cases and bags and half-opened stores and she resisted Ken's efforts to draw her in. Greg still stood in the doorway chewing gum and smiling nonchalantly. He was smug; he was confident and he had brought the right people here to tempt her back, not even waiting for a reply to his letter.

Fury rose in her and she turned to speak to Robert but he wasn't there. The car had gone, too. So he couldn't even wait for her. Men were all the same. They put on the charm when it suited and then let you down when you needed them.

She rushed off down the path shrugging off all attempts by the others to detain her and began to pace the short distance up the dark road to Dove

Cottage, oblivious to the chill wind on her bare arms or the painful stones pressing through her thin shoes. Tomorrow morning she would go round to see him early and tell him exactly what she thought of him for abandoning her when he was supposed to be taking her home.

★ ★ ★

Robert drove like a maniac back along the road, not knowing where he was going, then suddenly making a decision, he slapped on the brakes, made an abrupt turn and headed for the harbour. He couldn't face his cottage tonight. On his boat he would feel calmer, alone with his thoughts and feelings. He could raise the anchor at any time and be away, away from all the heartache, at one with the sea. Why was he letting her get to him this way?

He knew she was still in love with Greg, that this separation was only temporary, that she would go back to the theatre and to him. She belonged in a different world, not a tiny remote Scottish island. So why had it hit him so hard to see the man standing there? He didn't want her in his life anyway. He could never commit himself to another woman. He really did have to get a grip. The pain was tearing him apart.

When Vanessa arrived at his cottage next morning there was no sign of him. Angus drove up just as she had given up knocking on his door. 'I'm just bringing his car back, lass,' he said. 'Were you wanting anything?'

'I wanted to speak to him,' she said.

Angus smoothed his beard. 'Well now, he'll most likely be gone a wee while this time. He's instructed me to clear out all the food and lock his cottage up. That usually means he's away for a month or two.'

An unbearable emptiness was growing inside her.

'Where's he gone?'

'Well, I wouldn't know that. He's

maybe gone back home.'

'Don't you have an address?' she almost shouted.

'Och, no. He doesn't tell me his whereabouts. Maude Campbell would maybe tell you. She mostly sees to things when he's away.'

Panic was giving way to sadness. What did it matter where he'd gone? She was going herself on Saturday. But she wished they'd had time to talk and that they hadn't parted the way they had.

'I thought you'd finished with the children,' Audrey said as Vanessa rushed round getting her bag ready on Monday morning.

'I should have, but Fiona asked me if I'd help her to keep the drama group going. With no teacher yet the children are at home and the parents are trying to keep them occupied.'

'But, it's your holiday, dear. You should be relaxing. We're going home on Saturday and it's not been much of a rest for you.'

'I know, but they enjoyed working on

the play so much that they wanted to do another one.'

'But why are they expecting you to be there?'

Vanessa was irritable. 'I don't know, Mum. Everyone seems to assume I'll be there, help with a sort of holiday club for them while the teacher's ill. I don't seem to be able to disentangle myself from it.'

'Well, I don't think it's right. Robert ought to sort it out.'

'Mum, Robert isn't even on the island. Anyway, at least it keeps me out of Greg's way. He's hardly likely to come to the hall and pester me with all the children and mums there, is he?'

'Is he pestering you?' Audrey's voice showed concern.

'He's not very good at taking no for an answer. He always seems to get what he wants one way or another.'

'And have you definitely decided?'

'Not really. I need some thinking time. He wants me to produce their next play.'

'Is that what you want?'

'It would give me experience producing and I know I could make a success of it. There's such a lot of talent in that group.'

Audrey smiled. 'You're very fond of them, aren't you, dear? Friendship like that is very precious.'

'I'm comfortable with them. They've become almost like family. I really don't know what to do.'

'What about Greg?' her mother asked cautiously.

Vanessa sighed. 'He's the big problem.'

Audrey looked at her daughter. 'Be careful, dear. I don't want you getting hurt again.'

'But what else should I do? Producing jobs aren't ten a penny.'

'What about the agency? They've offered you some interesting work in the past when you've been thinking of moving on. Why not see what they have to offer?'

'That's true. It's just that if I produce

a really successful play with the Cheltern Players it will mean I have more to offer. Look, Mum, I have to get going, I promised I'd be there by ten. Can we talk tonight?'

Audrey smiled. Her daughter would make up her own mind in her own time.

Vanessa gave her mum a big hug and swung out of the door.

She had organised the children in groups and given them each a theme to work on with one of the mums in each group. Now the adults were having a coffee break in the back room while she had the children seated round her on the floor while she told them one of her much loved stories.

'You were a good Gingerbread Man, Vanessa,' Hannah told her.

'But she's a proper actress, isn't she?'

'I'm going to be an actress like Vanessa,' Emma piped up.

Jamie gave her a dismissive look. 'Don't be silly.'

'Jamie, that is not silly,' Vanessa scolded. 'I think any of you could be

113

anything you want to be. You just have to work hard at it. When I was little like you I knew what I wanted to do, so I went ahead and did it. So no more of that sort of talk.'

★　★　★

By lunchtime she was exhausted and just wanted to go home and relax. But Denise and Ken were outside waiting for her.

'You're coming back with us for a coffee,' Denise said taking her arm firmly. 'Greg is out sailing in the bay with Felicity. He won't be back for hours and if he does arrive we'll lock him out.'

Vanessa sighed and followed her two friends back to The Hole. Inside was a shambles of boots, waterproofs and clothes, the kitchen littered with opened tins and packets. Denise shrugged resignedly.

'I can't keep any semblance of order here. They refuse to tidy up, wash up or in any way co-operate in keeping the

114

place habitable so I give up. But I can manage a couple of coffees.'

Vanessa smiled at the familiar, good-natured ranting. It had always been like this. Plump and cuddly Denise was quite efficient, working in the background laundering, mending, ironing and improvising costumes on a minute budget. She could always be relied upon for advice, help and comfort.'

'I didn't know you were all into climbing and sailing, especially Greg,' Vanessa said, taking in all the gear lying around.

Ken stood with his back to the fire, short and stocky with slightly balding hair. As an older member of the group, Vanessa had always respected him and never tired of his strong deep voice with the lilting Welsh accent.

He smiled. 'Greg believes he can do anything. At least he is a strong swimmer and that is probably what he will end up doing when his boat capsizes. But, my dear, we are here simply to talk you into coming back.'

'It's a bit dramatic, isn't it, coming the length of the country to retrieve me? Why not have simply waited until I came home?'

'Because, my dear Vanessa, Greg Wilson does not do things in a simple manner. Besides we didn't know you were coming home. You did leave rather rapidly, disappearing to a remote Scottish island, with no forwarding address. You have no idea what difficulty Greg had in tracing you. Once you had moved on from here there would probably have been no way at all.'

He sat beside her and took her hand.

'Will you come back with us? It's very important to the group and it's a good opportunity for you.'

Denise put a mug of coffee in her hand and stood back surveying her and trying to assess her reaction. Vanessa drank the coffee thoughtfully. Then she looked up at them.

'Greg wrote to me, you know. He doesn't just want me back with the group, he wants me back with him.'

Denise nodded. 'I know. He's been like a bear with a sore head since you left. He had a blazing row with Mandy and blamed her for everything. She threw one of her tantrums and went off in a blaze of glory. I can tell you it's been a pantomime and no mistaking.'

Vanessa smiled. Familiar scenes were flooding her memory, not all unhappy, and she felt vindicated that Mandy West had had her comeuppance.

'I won't go back with Greg though. It all hurt too much and I've lost respect for him now, and trust. It couldn't work again.'

'Look, love, we appreciate your position and we understand if you feel you can't come back. You must think about it carefully.'

'I came here to think; that was the whole idea.'

'Yes, I know, but Greg was going to come alone and drag you back, so we decided it would be better if we all came. It wasn't exactly as if we were busy.'

'So what has been going on with the theatre since I left?'

'Nothing, in fact we've been kicking our heels and wondering what to do since the end of the last production. It's lucky the theatre was booked up for the puppet show.'

'But why haven't you started on something new, if Greg's back and you have a good group together again?'

'Because we need you back with us, otherwise everything will fold and we'll all be out of work. They don't trust Greg anymore after he let us all down so badly. You bring in the audiences and we know you'll be able to produce this new play as well as act in it. You rescued the last show. We know you can do it.'

Vanessa felt a warm glow of pride, knowing how much she was needed by her friends.

'I'm not persuading you against your will,' Denise continued. 'All I will say is that if you decide to come back we'll give you all the support you need both in the production and against any

118

harassment from Greg.'

'I don't think Vanessa fears Greg's advances as much as she fears her own feelings,' Ken said.

Vanessa gave him a weak smile. He was right.

A Terrifying Encounter
At Sea

By Friday she had still not decided. 'Vanessa, we really do need to know what's happening. Are you to come with us tomorrow, or are we to leave you here and drive back alone?' Geoff was irritable at her indecision.

Vanessa wished people wouldn't keep pushing her.

'No, Dad, please don't worry. I won't let you down. But couldn't we all stay for just a few days longer?'

Audrey intervened. 'Of course, love, we don't have anything to rush back for and the cottage seems to be ours for as long as we want it. Come on, Geoff; let's just relax for a few more days. It is lovely here and we may not get another chance to come back in a hurry.'

Geoff sighed. 'I suppose another

couple of days won't do any harm.'

'When are your friends leaving?' her mother asked.

'I don't know.' It was the truth and she feared they would not leave until they had a firm decision from her. Besides which, Greg had taken a liking to sailing and was off every day with Felicity in one of the hired dinghies.

As she walked to the hall for another session with the children her mind was in a turmoil. She could simply stay put on the island, let them all go and leave her here to sort out her future in peace. One of them would drive her parents back home. The cottage was cheap; in fact she could probably live free if she agreed to continue doing drama and music sessions with the children. The relief teacher, when she did arrive, would probably be grateful for a little assistance in that direction. The parents were appreciative of her efforts even if Robert wasn't.

Round and round in circles her mind went. The children needed her, the theatre needed her.

'But what do you need?' Denise had asked her several times during the week.

'I don't know,' she admitted. Something was holding her back, nagging at her subconscious, something she didn't want to acknowledge.

The children were particularly restless during the session. Jamie was unusually mischievous, demanding more than his fair share of attention, and Emma was hot and flushed so that Vanessa felt sure she was coming down with something. Hannah was particularly bossy and hit little Sam across the face. Fiona was the only mum to turn up to help her and she was busy giving Angus the order for supplies when he went over to the mainland later that day.

Finally Vanessa lost patience and snapped at them, a thing she had never done before and they looked at her in astonishment, immediately sitting down on the floor as she had asked them to do. Her nerves were frayed with the tensions of the past days and needed an outlet.

'I shan't be coming in any more after today. Your new teacher should be here any day now and you'll all be back at school.'

Twelve little upturned faces stared at her in disbelief. Jamie and Hannah quickly sobered and Emma's face began to crumple until tears welled out. Hannah put a comforting arm round her. They were absolutely silent and sat immobile, eventually turning their eyes away and down to the floor.

Vanessa watched them, her heart thudding and her emotions raw. She loved them all dearly and now due to her own taut nerves she had taken it out on them because they were too young to answer back. She swallowed hard and walked over to Jamie; he had always been her favourite. As she crouched down to his level, his round face looked up at her, his eyes serious.

'If we're very good will you stay 'til Mrs McPhearson comes back?'

Fighting back tears she put her arms round him and kissed the top of his curly head. 'Yes,' she agreed, knowing she was making a foolish commitment.

★ ★ ★

On her way home she decided to call in at The Hole to tell Denise she had made her decision. She would consider producing the next play and try to get the group on its feet again but not for a few weeks yet. She was enjoying working with the children and she had unfinished business of another nature to attend to.

As she approached The Hole it was quiet but the door stood open and there was the sound of dishes clinking in the kitchen. She popped her head in and called out.

The noise stopped and then to her surprise Greg came sauntering through the living-room, tea-towel in hand.

He grinned at her charmingly. 'I'm afraid Denise is out walking. Ken and Felicity are replenishing stores and I've been left in charge of dishes. No dishes, no dinner! With an ultimatum like that how could I refuse? You wouldn't like to help, would you?' he asked, winking at her.

She found herself smiling at his impudence. It was as if nothing had changed; that he had not broken her heart by having an affair with another woman. But that was Greg.

'I thought you'd have been out sailing,' she said.

'I was going but Felicity thought it was too windy and I don't care to sail single handed, not yet anyway until I'm more competent. It's a fantastic sport though. You ought to try it.'

'I have,' she said.

His eyes widened. 'You mean you can sail. I didn't know that.'

'I used to sail with Dad when I was young. He had a yacht, but Mum didn't care for it much, so as I got older and had less time he sold it. I haven't sailed at all since then.'

He was getting very excited now, talking rapidly and rushing around the room.

'We'll go sailing right now. Here, Vanessa, try these waterproofs for size. They fit Felicity so they should fit you. We could get a couple hours in before dinner. You come with me, won't you?' he asked as an afterthought.

She shook her head and backed away. The attraction was still there and she couldn't trust herself with him. When he saw she was preparing to leave he leapt to her side and slid an arm round her.

'Vanessa, please don't go. Come and talk to me. If you don't want to sail, fine. Stupid of me.'

She looked at him, his bright eyes wildly darting, the almost white blond hair, his smooth brown arms. His touch still excited her and she wanted to stay with him, even if just for the familiarity of knowing him so well. However badly he had treated her she could not dislike him. At least he always made her feel wanted.

Greg became more serious. 'I meant what I said in the letter. I know I've treated you badly, Vanessa. But as I told you when it happened, Mandy meant nothing to me, none of the others did.'

'I don't think anyone means that much to you, Greg,' she said.

His arm tightened round her waist. 'You do, darling. Please come back to me. I'll try very hard to be faithful.'

She shook her head. 'I'll think about coming back to the Cheltern and producing the next play, but I can't come back to you, Greg. Our relationship is over and you've got to accept that. Will you promise me you won't make things difficult if I do come back?'

She released herself from his grip and looked him straight in the eye. He was about to protest and she silenced him.

'I mean it. If you pester me or make things difficult I shall walk out, whatever happens to the production or the company, if you don't toe the line I shall abandon ship and leave you all to it, I promise.'

He put his hands up in mock surrender. 'Do I have a choice?'

'No,' she said firmly. 'And I'm only thinking about it, so don't get too excited.'

She still wasn't sure she could work with Greg on a professional level. Once she was back in that very claustrophobic atmosphere created in a repertory theatre, when tension was high and everything depended on getting a show together, would she be able to resist his advances?

He still had the waterproof jacket in his hand and was now looking down at it despondently. A surge of pity sprang up in her.

'Do you really want to go sailing?'

He looked surprised, and then a grin transformed his face.

'You're going to come with me? You are!' He leapt in the air. 'Darling, you're wonderful.'

★ ★ ★

They scrambled down the cliff to the cove where Greg had moored the hired

128

dinghy. The sea was choppy, she felt light-hearted suddenly and in a real holiday mood.

She smiled at Greg. 'Friends again?'

He squeezed her arm.

She helped him launch the small boat, then waded out into the cold water and hopped in beside him.

'You take the helm and I'll unfurl the sails,' she told him.

'Aye, aye, Skipper,' he teased.

The sails were soon caught up by the gusting wind and Vanessa put all her strength into holding them. Greg grabbed the tiller but his inexperience made it difficult for her to predict the tacking. She reefed the sails to gain more control and they soon had the craft skimming the water at an exhilarating speed. She glanced back at Greg's earnest face, spray splashed, his hair whipping across his eyes as sun filtered through scudding clouds and glinted tantalisingly on the surf.

'I don't know how you and Felicity managed,' Vanessa teased. 'Must have been the blind leading the blind.'

He agreed obligingly, 'It was, only conditions were a little less hairy. In fact there was so little wind the first time, we had to row back. Much more fun this way.'

She smiled at him. 'It's good to be together again. I have missed you.'

'We always were good together,' he said.

'We did have some good times.' She gave him a wistful smile.

Their eyes met and her heart twisted painfully.

'We still could.' He was holding her gaze.

'Maybe.' She was tempted.

A gust took the sails and they both had to put all their effort into keeping the yacht on course. Skimming the waves, the yacht hit each one and bounced over it, salt water spraying their faces until their hair hung dripping. It was fun, it was exhilarating and they shouted out and shrieked with laughter as each wave hit them.

Vanessa leapt from side to side to try to control the sails, ducking to avoid the boon swinging across with violent force. She was happier than she had been for a long time. She settled herself beside Greg at the helm, still holding the sail in tight trim.

He slipped his arm round her shoulder. 'Vanessa, I'm sorry about what's happened, what I did to you. I didn't mean to hurt you, never would have done.' He paused. 'It's just me, I suppose. Unstable, unreliable. I'll never make anyone a good husband.'

She smiled up at him. 'You're a brilliant actor, though.' There was a moment as their eyes met when she felt the old longing, then his attention was distracted again as he steered round a small outcrop of rock.

'Yes. I've thought it all out. I'm no good at producing, not able to cope with people, that's the trouble. But acting is different. That's what I'm going to work at, take my opportunities and who knows — maybe the neon

131

signs will spell my name in the not too distant future.'

He took her hand and squeezed it gently, looking at her with compassion. 'Why don't you take over from me and run the Cheltern Players. You'll make a go of it, I know you will.'

Storm clouds were gathering and Vanessa gave an involuntary shiver. A great gust nearly ripped the rope from her hand as the sail tore angrily taut. Greg straightened to brace himself against the wind and hold the boat on course. Spray soaked them as stronger waves lashed the boat's side.

'I think we ought to head back.' Greg's voice was tight with apprehension.

Vanessa struggled to reef the sails ever further. 'Just hold her on this course,' she yelled at him.

They were battling against the tide and she had brief misgivings about her chances of manoeuvring the boat safely back but quickly dispelled them. Greg was strong, if a little inexperienced.

'Hold on, watch that boat!' she yelled.

She had been so busy adjusting the sails and ropes and working out their best approach to land that when the large bulk of a fishing boat loomed ahead of them it took her completely by surprise. Greg had been watching her activities and marvelling at her expertise so had not noticed the oncoming vessel himself.

'Greg, turn her! Watch the boom! Duck!' There was no point in using boating language, as there was a chance Greg wouldn't understand or respond quickly enough.

Vanessa jumped to the helm and quickly grabbed the tiller from him, heaving on the ropes and ducking to miss the boom all in one well-practiced manoeuvre. The dinghy did an about turn and Greg was left dazed and hanging to the side for grim death.

An angry voice shouted something which was lost to the stormy sea and Vanessa was aware only of a green clad fisherman shaking his arms at her.

When they recovered stability Vanessa remained at the helm and instructed Greg on exactly what to do.

'Close one there,' he mumbled, trying not to sound too shaken.

Vanessa was silent, suddenly aware of their precarious position. Rain was beginning to deluge the boat and the skies became ominously dark. She decided on her plan and was intent now only on making sure Greg did exactly what was required for them to reach the jetty safely. She just wished they hadn't come so far out and that they weren't sailing against the tide.

Another frightening thought subdued her. 'Greg, where are the lifejackets?'

'I don't know, I don't think we have any,' he yelled back, panic in his face.

As she moved on to a long straight tack she noticed the fishing boat moving across her bow forcing her to change her direction again.

'Engines should give way to sails,' she yelled.

Greg stared at the fishing boat as it doubled back again forcing them to change direction. 'It almost seems as though that lout is provoking us.'

Vanessa was becoming more and more agitated, trying to keep control of the dinghy and at the same time predict the movements of the larger craft.

'He's forcing us into the coast,' she said, alarmed. 'He'll have us up on the rocks. What is he playing at?'

Try as she would, she could not out-manoeuvre the other boat and at times the two came perilously near to a collision. She was vaguely aware of a human voice calling through the tumult but gave up trying to make any sense of the sound.

She tacked and manoeuvred the dinghy and it took every atom of her wit and energy to avoid colliding with the ever-pursuing larger boat. As the jutting rocks loomed nearer, fear gripped her stomach as she anticipated the crunch of wood and the cold reality of that icy water. And what then? Who was this lunatic and what did he want?

The waves were lashing them up near to the rocks and then, as the sea receded, it took them, too. The fishing boat stayed close making any manoeuvre to get away impossible. Greg worked beside Vanessa trying to catch on to what she wanted but he was out of his depth and she could see fear in his face as well as annoyance and puzzlement as to what was happening.

The fishing boat came up behind them then and forced Vanessa to steer out round a jutting rock and she cringed as a wave took the dinghy out just far enough to avoid it. As the two boats came closer she could see the man in the green again; his sou'wester pulled down over his head to keep out the beating wind and rain.

She was soaked to the skin and her fingers were aching with cold, her thin trousers and shirt clinging to her where spray had run down the neck of the waterproof jacket and her feet squelched in the water at the bottom of the dinghy.

136

Still she couldn't hear what the fisherman was shouting and Greg leaned over and cupped his ear to try to catch some words.

'I think he wants to throw us a rope,' he said.

The man did have a coil of rope in his hands. And now Vanessa could make out another figure standing inside the wheelhouse. Then all her concentration was needed again to control the dinghy, and relief suddenly flooded her as she saw, just to the lee of the rocky outcrop, a small flat beach sloping gently up to a large overhang of rock. She steered directly for it and with the help of another wave managed to ground the dinghy with a final crunch.

Greg was out of the boat in an instant and heaving on its hull to get it farther up the beach and away from any chance wave which may re-float it.

Vanessa sat down in the boat, breathing deeply to try to gain control of her nerves and stop the whole of her body from violently shaking.

Suddenly a pair of arms lifted her straight out and on to the beach and she found herself looking into those now familiar eyes. Robert's face was like thunder and his grip on her arms made her want to shout out in pain.

'What the devil were you playing at?' he growled at her.

She was too exhausted and too relieved to answer and felt her legs giving under her. Greg came forward to argue but Robert scowled at him and flung Vanessa to him and Greg caught her in his arms. Robert marched back down the beach to where a small wooden rowing boat was casually hooked up to a wooden post, the fishing boat moored just a little way out in the bay bobbing violently on its anchor chain. He pointed to the boat and looked back to where Greg still stood numbed, holding Vanessa.

'Well, do you want to walk back or come with me? You're not sailing that dinghy,' he growled. Then to prove his point he walked to the dinghy and at an opportune moment, when a wave caught it, he heaved at the bow and sent it crashing back into the sea.

Vanessa watched as the small boat tossed farther and farther from the shore and became increasingly sure that Robert must be mad. He scowled back at her questioningly and though her arms and legs ached and she was wet through, nothing would have persuaded her to go back in the fishing boat. She turned to Greg.

'We'll walk.'

He was still stunned by the whole episode and looked at her in every greater amazement at this suggestion.

'Vanessa, it's miles. We can't walk in all this wet gear.'

She pulled away from him and shrugged.

'Please yourself, but I'm going to.'

He looked from Robert to Vanessa and then back to where Robert still stood at the water's edge, and then he turned and ran after Vanessa who was now scrambling up the cliffs from the beach to the higher road.

It was a nail breaking, rugged climb up sheer rock face and only extreme anger and the knowledge that Robert was watching drove Vanessa on. Face to face with grey wet rock she clung and heaved her aching body with a grim determination to escape that patronising stare. The whole of her being was driving her on beyond endurance as if a mad frenzy possessed her.

'Hold on!' She was brought back to reality by Greg's shriek from behind. Looking down, whilst still clinging to a rugged ledge of rock with her back pressed hard into a hollow cavity, she watched him struggling to remove his flapping waterproof jacket which was hindering progress.

Eventually he caught up with her and stood enveloping her body from the unrelenting wind and rain and for a moment she relaxed in the shelter he provided.

'We're crazy doing this, you know,' he breathed through numb lips, water dripping from his hair and running down his face. 'What got into you? That bloke was only trying to help us out, you know. Why couldn't we have gone back with him?'

Vanessa leaned her head against him, grateful that he had not deserted her.

'We have to carry on,' she breathed, fearful that her aching muscles would seize up completely before safety was reached.

'Come on, old girl, we'll make it,' he encouraged.

Greg's easy encouragement somehow got them to the plateau from where a narrow worn path gave promise of survival.

Pausing on the grassy ledge, Vanessa looked down in horror at the drop below them.

'He's still on the beach looking up. He hasn't moved, not one step,' she said.

'Who is he?' Greg had been so concerned with reaching safety, the thought had only just occurred to him.

'Do you know him?'

Though Vanessa could not see Robert's face she felt the penetration of those eyes and knew the look he gave as he turned now to his rowing boat and the still lashing sea. She watched as he unhooked it and battled against the wind and waves to row back to his fishing boat.

'Yes, I know him,' she sighed.

Greg gave her a quizzical look.

* * *

It was a long, uphill walk and even Greg's exuberant nature was beginning to flag as they plodded along, still dripping wet and hampered by their wet clothing.

'So, who is he?' Greg persisted.

Vanessa shrugged wearily. 'He's just a fisherman who lives here,' was all she could manage.

Greg shook his head and gave her a hug. 'Well, he's a lunatic, that's all I can say. Come on, cheer up, we're nearly back. Look, there's your cottage. Shall I come in with you?'

She gave him a weak smile. 'No, you get back and dry off. I'll be fine now. And thanks.'

Audrey was coming through from the kitchen with a pile of books stacked in a cardboard box and almost dropped them when she saw the state of her daughter.

'What on earth?' she began, and Vanessa silenced her.

'Mum, I can't explain now. But I've made my decision. I'm not going back with you. Denise will drive you home on Wednesday when they go. I've things to settle, a lot of things to sort out.'

'Just think, dear, about what you're getting into this time, won't you?' she said, and Vanessa wished that thinking would solve any of her problems, as the more she thought things through, the more confused she became.

★   ★   ★

'Vanessa, I don't like to leave you here alone.' The anxious words brought Vanessa from a troubled sleep and she winced as she tried to lift herself up in the bed to take the morning tea her mother was offering.

'But, Mum, you're not leaving yet. You said you'd stay a few more days. I want to arrange for Denise to drive you back.'

Audrey perched on the bed beside her as she sipped the comforting drink. 'No, dear, we have to leave in half an hour for the ferry, then we'll pick the car up in Mallaig. Your dad wants to get back. You know how restless he gets these days if he can't keep on the move.'

'But who's going to drive.'

'Dad wants to. He's quite capable now, and I think it will do him good, restore his confidence. We may stay a night or two en-route. We passed through some very interesting places coming up.'

Vanessa was worried but felt too

weak to argue. Everyone must just do what they wanted to. She couldn't be responsible for everything. Her mum was right.

Audrey continued. 'I'd be much happier if you came with us. You will come back with the others, won't you, otherwise, how will you get back?'

'Mum, there are trains.'

'Do think about it. What have you to stay for? Come home with us and give yourself a real holiday and time to think things over before moving on. I know you have your career to think about, but it will be much easier once you're back where you belong.'

As she opened her mouth to speak, a searing pain shot down her cheek and she felt the graze and swelling and re-membered banging it against an outcrop of rock on her ascent from the beach yesterday.

'I'll be all right, honestly, Mum. I like this island. I've made friends here and I want to carry on with the children for a while. I do find it quite therapeutic. It will do me more good than moping around at home with nothing to do and I'm not ready to make any big moves towards my future just yet. Really, I'll be fine.'

★   ★   ★

Vanessa searched the island for Robert, eventually tracking him down in the old school room searching through cupboards, stacking books and generally reorganising the room.

When he heard her footsteps he looked round, surprised at seeing her. Quickly he regained his composure, obviously unsure whether to assume indifference or pursue yesterday's episode.

Vanessa gave him no choice, plunging straight in with a release of all the pent up frustration of the night.

'I'd like an explanation for your superb display yesterday. Whatever your silly game was about, I found it extremely offensive, if not positively dangerous.'

'Not half as dangerous as the game

you were playing,' he said in a controlled voice. He closed the cupboard door and walked towards her.

'What do you mean?' she snapped.

'You were out in the dinghy with no safety equipment, not even a life jacket. The weather made it inadvisable to be out at sea in any small craft yesterday especially when you have little knowledge of these waters and even less knowledge of handling a boat.'

She could have hit him and her eyes flashed fury.

'And what gives you the right to decide how capable I am? Besides, what you did was far more dangerous, forcing me into the coast. Do you realise the boat almost smashed up on the rocks? Which brings me to the point of my visit. Who do you suppose is going to explain the loss of the dinghy and more to the point who is going to pay for it? Greg hired it, which makes it legally his responsibility, but without your harassment we might just have got it back in one piece. Now, due to your highhanded behaviour it's lost and I don't see why we should pay for that loss.'

He put up a hand to stave off her onslaught. 'Vanessa, I take full responsibility for the loss of the boat. That has never been in question. I apologise for frightening you yesterday. I can assure you that if there had been another way I would have taken it. The weather made it impossible for you to hear my warnings and I knew you were in danger. Unlike you, I do have expert knowledge of weather conditions and tides round this coast. I also know the coastline precisely.'

Here he stopped and looked at her knowingly, forcing her to remember the first afternoon when they had sheltered from the storm in the hidden cave. He continued, never once taking his eyes from her face. 'And unlike you, again, I did have the expertise with a boat to guide you to the safety of the beach. There may have been some danger of you damaging the boat on the cliffs but that was of little concern to me, as you know.'

Her blood was boiling at his arrogance. 'No, it wouldn't matter to you, would it? You go around as if you own this island, interfering in people's lives. Maybe the islanders like that. You're the champion of their cause, the big chief. Well, don't think you can interfere in my life.'

'I wouldn't dream of it,' he said with irritating calm, but the muscles in his face showed he was fighting for control.

'And don't think I'm staying on to suit your purposes, I'm doing it for the children because I've promised them. If it wasn't for them I'd have been away this morning with my parents.'

He shook his head and sighed.

'I'm sorry you didn't leave with them. I did try to get a message through to you but obviously the jungle telegraph isn't terribly efficient in these parts.'

'What message?' she asked, her fury subsiding rapidly.

'I brought the replacement school teacher with me yesterday. That was the purpose of my journey. So it won't be necessary for you to spend any more time with them. They will be back at school full time on Monday morning. No more time for fun and games and stories.'

'What do you mean? It was not just fun and games as you put it. And you were very glad of my help when Hettie was taken ill.'

'That's right. Thank you, Vanessa, for helping out. I know everyone is very grateful to you, especially for seeing the concert through.'

'You're dismissing me, just like that?'

'I thought it was what you wanted.'

'Yes,' she said in a very small voice.

She swallowed hard to try to gain control. Her legs felt weak and a terrible emptiness threatened to overtake her. She was being dismissed, cast aside. Now that she was no longer useful to him he didn't care how soon she went, even if he didn't see her again.

'Perhaps you could leave with your friends on Wednesday. At least you would have company on the journey.'

He sounded so cold and formal and she couldn't believe it was the same man who had taken her in his arms and cooked for her and told her how beautiful she was. Try as she would the tears were coming. His deep, dark eyes still looked down at her, drawing her to him. She wanted him to pull her close, show somehow that he cared, but he stood there firmly in control.

Then he turned as a tall, blonde woman walked into the room and in a loud, confident voice greeted him. He smiled and shook hands with the woman. 'This is Miss Hughes, our temporary teacher.'

She nodded at Vanessa. 'Oh, dear, you do look a mess. Whatever happened?'

Not waiting for a reply she took in the room then turned to Robert. 'Strange little place, isn't it. I suppose these island children are an odd bunch, too. Hardly seems worth sending me so far for twelve children.'

Vanessa stared from Robert to the new teacher and back to Robert and felt she could take no more. Robert caught her eye just as she turned to leave and saw the first tears wetting her cheek. He moved to stop her then hesitated and turned back into the room. Vanessa rushed out and down the road, not wanting to go back to her empty cottage, not knowing where she did want to go.

After showing Cynthia Hughes round the school, Robert left as quickly as good manners would allow. He wanted to be on his own to nurse his deep dejection. Why was he treating her this way?

So, she had gone out in the dinghy and got into trouble. Actually she had managed it extremely well and probably would have made it safely into the harbour if he had not interfered.

Why was he so intent on putting her down? But he knew the answer. It was just his way, the way his family dealt with people, the way his father had treated them; it was in his blood.

He would have to apologise to her and try to explain. He owed her that. He couldn't just leave her thinking how rude and insensitive he was. But after that he would leave her alone. He would not hurt her again.

* * *

Mists swirled round the high peaks and damp cold air clung to her face as Vanessa made her way up the winding road. She wasn't sure why she was making for the old church but it seemed a suitable place to nurse her depression.

Wild garlic lined the path and filled the air with its delicate smell. Splashes of yellow iris gave brilliant contrast to the green landscape of hills and the stark brown of the mountains.

The church ahead stood alone and grey in the distance, mist swirling and clearing tantalisingly, giving hidden glimpses of dark craggy heights and then shielding them again in fluffy whiteness. Misty Island, she thought. It would always be that to her, not Brae or the ancient Gaelic name Robert gave it, rolling the sounds softly off his tongue.

The old wooden gate creaked when she pushed it open, speaking of age and mystery. Inside the crumbling grey stone building were wooden pews worn smooth with centuries of worship. It was quiet and cold so that Vanessa pulled her jacket to, shivered and quickly moved outside where the mist was swirling lower and encircling the tombstones.

Some were so lofty and ornate, their inscription telling of lives long gone. Amidst the more ostentatious memorials were simple slabs of stone and wooden crosses; two graves over in a corner bore only a rough lump of granite where some poor soul had been laid to rest.

Idling among memories of the past

Vanessa felt a certain peace until she came across a small, modern grave with a simple marble cross, the lettering in gold. She had been drawn to it by the vase of primroses placed carefully in its centre and a cold dread filled her as she read the words.

Helen McKenzie, dearly loved wife of Robert. Joe, aged eight, their son. Both lost at sea.

She read the date. Four years ago. She couldn't read anymore, instinctively knowing that was Robert's family, a wife and son, both dead and he hadn't told her.

She tore her eyes away from the black marble and on shaking legs forced herself out of the churchyard and down the road, willing her legs to go faster, forcing her breathing to remain calm.

These were the woman and child in the photo. He still grieved for them; it explained so much. What had happened to them? What terrible tragedy had left him so bereft?

When she reached her cottage she

slammed the door and gave vent to tearful sobs aware only that deep inside her was an aching void.

The last person she expected to have as a visitor that afternoon was Hettie. The cheerful round lady was a shade paler than Vanessa remembered her at the ceilidh, but otherwise looked well.

'I'm a sight better now I'm back on the island,' she told her, settling into a comfy chair. Vanessa felt her heart lift at the cheerful voice. She was like a breath of fresh air coming in.

They had tea and biscuits and Vanessa related every detail of every child since Hettie had taken ill until they came to the real purpose of Hettie's visit.

The lady's face crumpled as she confided to Vanessa, 'This new one, she won't do at all.'

Vanessa tried to reassure her. 'But it will only be for a couple of weeks. You'll be able to take over again after the holiday.

Hettie shook her head. 'Could you not stay on a wee while longer? The bairns have taken to you.'

Vanessa felt a warm comfort from this compliment but knew it was impossible. 'Hettie, they will be back at school on Monday. There won't be time for my sessions with them. I was only really helping with the concert, and then it just drifted into a drama session, just keeping them occupied.'

'Poppycock!' Hettie exclaimed. 'That young lady does not want to teach here, she does not want to be here. I am sure she would not object to a little assistance,' she suggested conspiratorially and Vanessa had to laugh.

'No, I suppose that might work. But I'm going home on Wednesday.'

Hettie watched her critically, her small eyes seeking deeply into Vanessa's secrets. Vanessa badly wanted to talk to her, feeling a depth of understanding in the elderly lady.

'Is Robert chasing you away?' Hettie asked.

Vanessa started at the direction of the question. 'No, not at all. My friends are going so I may as well join them. I have nothing to stay for.'

'No?' The question had a perceptiveness that was difficult to ignore.

Hettie leaned across and patted her knee. 'My dear, I hear the gossip. My goodness, on this island what else is there to do?'

'What gossip?' Vanessa interrupted.

'Now don't get cross. Women visitors are always falling madly in love with our Robert, but he doesn't usually pay them any attention. I have heard he's been paying you quite a lot.'

'He's been friendly,' Vanessa said. 'There's nothing more to it. Besides, he's hardly been here. As far as I can see he spends most of his time bobbing backwards and forwards between the mainland and the island.'

Hettie nodded reflectively. 'Yes, poor boy. He'd rather stay put here on the island, but they won't let him be, always trying to win him back to the fold.'

'What, you mean his parents won't allow him to live his own life as he pleases?' Vanessa said.

'Well, it's not quite that simple. He's been at loggerheads with his family for years. They don't see things his way and he won't succumb to their demands.'

Vanessa was only half listening: family feuds were common enough. The mystery she had uncovered that afternoon was foremost in her mind and she was wondering how she could approach the subject with Hettie without appearing to fuel her suspicions about their relationship. Hettie made the exercise unnecessary.

'Of course that dreadful tragedy changed him. He was a real fighter before, then afterwards it was years before he took any interest again in anything.'

'What happened?' Vanessa asked.

Hettie raised her eyebrows. 'You don't know? Hasn't he told you? Well, now, I suppose he might not. It must still be very painful, especially for someone as sensitive and self contained as Robert.'

She leant over conspiratorially. 'His wife and son were drowned. She was a sweet wee girl, and the loveliest boy you ever saw. Joe was one of my most promising pupils; came from a good line you see, plenty of intelligence and good breeding on the McKenzie side.

'Not that they would acknowledge him. As far as they were concerned the child didn't exist, the marriage didn't exist. But Robert didn't care. He was besotted by the sweet girl. Very like Morag, she was. I've rarely seen two sisters more alike, almost like twins only Helen was two years older.'

Pieces were slotting together as she spoke and Vanessa was filled with dreadful conflicting emotions. There were stirrings of pity, an overwhelming longing to reach out to Robert, combining with a fear of rejection. She was still convinced that his heart lay firmly elsewhere, and the safest thing for her to do was to stick to her plans and go home and leave well alone.

Yet she couldn't resist finding out more. 'How did it happen?' she asked tentatively.

Hettie appeared to be lost in recollection. 'It was a dreadful day, early spring with storms and lashing rain. The children arrived at school soaked to the skin and I had to change their socks and rub them down. There was no teaching that morning. Joe McKenzie hadn't turned up and I hadn't had word about him being ill so we all worried and wondered about him.'

Vanessa hung on every word now, intent on finding out the full story. But Hettie was not to be hurried.

'He was a lovely boy, his father's dark curly hair, big wide eyes like his mother.' Hettie closed her eyes against the pain.

'It was mid afternoon and the rain was still lashing. The children were restless and it was getting so dark I was worried abut them getting home safely. Some have a way to walk home at the end of the day.'

She paused and smiled indulgently and then the pain was there again.

'I was about to close the school early and take the young ones back home myself when up in the sky we heard the helicopter. Then Fiona rushed into the classroom and told me they were searching for a boat, that Morag had seen it going out, and that wee Joe was in it with his mother and that Robert was beside himself, and the whole island was in turmoil. It was dreadful.'

Then Hettie was silent, battling with emotions long buried.

'But what happened?' Vanessa asked gently.

'Drowned. The boat was found wrecked. Robert was in a terrible state. Nobody could go near him for weeks. He would rage and curse and then he just shut himself up in his cottage.'

Hettie was struggling with her sorrow and Vanessa became worried that she may upset herself too much and put back her recovery.

'Look, let me make you some more tea,' Vanessa said kindly.

She took the cup of tea Vanessa

offered, her hand shaking. 'Thank you, dear. You know you would do him a world of good.'

Vanessa smiled. 'I'm going home on Wednesday.'

'Oh, that's a shame. I hear your friends are all of the acting profession. I was hoping they might have been persuaded to do a little turn for us at the ceilidh hall. I missed the concert, and we have so little chance here of entertainment.'

As she talked an idea was forming in Vanessa's mind, an absurd but nevertheless exciting plan.

'You won't be able to stay on then and help out. I was hoping you'd maybe just do some drama with the children and let this Miss *whatever-she's-called* teach them their sums and spellings. The wee things wouldn't feel so abandoned then. I know they've taken to you fine.'

Hettie rose to leave. 'You're a sweet girl and I'll be very sorry to see you go. And so should Robert be if he had any sense. Young people can be so obstinate.'

A germ of an idea was nudging its way into Vanessa's mind.

'Hettie, maybe I will stay on a little longer. I do love being here and I have enjoyed working with the children. But I'll have to think it through.'

'Oh, that would be lovely. But you must do what you feel is right for you, dear. Don't make any hasty decisions. You come and see me whenever you want.'

Vanessa watched as the elderly lady to the hill with practiced steps, halting for breath every few paces. Then she went back into the cottage feeling more hopeful than she had done for a very long time.

The Truth About Robert Emerges

'You're completely mad!' Greg threw his arms dramatically in the air.

They had been preparing a meal in the kitchen when Vanessa banged on the door of The Hole. Now they were gathered round her listening to the idea she had come up with whilst talking to Hettie half an hour earlier.

'You mean you want us all to move up here?' Felicity cried. 'Where would we live? And what would we live on? They're as poor as church mice. Who would pay?'

Denise came in. 'She's got a point, Vanessa. Where would the money come from to finance such a scheme?'

Vanessa shook her head. 'I honestly don't know. I haven't thought it through yet. It was just an idea that came to me and I wanted to sound you out. I suppose we would have to try to get a grant from somewhere or other and take very little ourselves at first.'

'Count me out,' Greg wailed. 'I'm not working for charity. Anyway, what a life. You don't seriously envisage a group traipsing from island to island on smelly fishing boats entertaining a handful of highlanders in a ceilidh hall, do you?'

Vanessa sighed. 'I had hoped you'd be a bit more enthusiastic.'

Denise was still frowning. 'It could be done. I'd have to think about it more, go into the figures.' Vanessa jumped up and hugged her.

'Now don't get carried away. I will think about it and I'll make some enquiries. We'd need to advertise for more people, form a new group. Her face was brightening. 'I do like the idea. It's very original.'

Greg was viewing them both with dismay. 'What about our play? What am I to do? I don't want any part of this scheme.'

Vanessa watched the panic in his eyes. 'You'll be fine, Greg. You could get a part in any company tomorrow and you know it. You're a good actor and you'll never be out of work for long.'

'But I want my company, the one I started, the one I built up. I want my play. I want to play Prospero. We could build it up together, Vanessa. You promised. You can't back out now, break up my company to form your own.'

Vanessa watched his face crumple into a spoilt pout and wanted to hug him. He really was very vulnerable.

'I didn't promise, Greg, and anyway we could do The Tempest as our first production. You can play Prospero,' she reassured him. 'This will be a new start for all of us. Please consider it.'

'Right, Felicity,' he said rising abruptly to his full six feet. 'We leave on Wednesday as planned and get back to the theatre and talk to the crew before they are all whisked off.'

'Not so fast,' Felicity said. 'I'm getting interested. The Cheltern Players are in trouble and you know it.'

'But our new production will get us back on form, I know it will,' Greg lamented.

'I think we have a better chance reforming and trying our luck up here,' Felicity said. 'I'd give it a go. I have nothing to go back for and I like it here.'

Vanessa could hardly contain her growing excitement yet the hurt look of defeat on Greg's face tore at her heart. She did still love and care about him.

'Greg, please consider it. If it doesn't work out we can all go back to Brighton. At least we will have tried.'

But he stood his ground. 'And what will we go back to? No, not under any circumstances. I will continue alone if I have to. The Cheltern Players will survive.'

Vanessa realised she was wasting her time trying to persuade him. But her mind was set now. With or without any of her friends she would produce a professional group and perform plays in all these isolated islands and bring the theatre to people.

* ★ ★ ★

During the next couple of days her mind was full of plans. The others were to go back on Wednesday as arranged leaving Vanessa on the island to prepare for their return in a few weeks.

She hadn't seen Robert since leaving him at the school, yet in quiet moments her mind had gone over and over what Hettie had told her, and the grave in the churchyard was imprinted on her mind.

When he appeared at her cottage on Tuesday evening she was just putting a light to the logs in the fireplace to ward off the evening chill. As she opened the door and saw him standing there, his eyes darkly serious, it was all she could do to stop herself from pulling him to her and hugging all the hurt from him. Yet she knew that it was not what he wanted.

Memory of their last encounter in the school flooded her with embarrassment as he followed her through to the shadowy room where the quickly growing flames cast mysterious shadows up the wall.

'I'm just trying to get a fire going. Would you like a drink?' she asked.

Relief emanated from him as if he had been expecting a difficult time and was pleased to find hospitality instead. He forced an uneasy smile. 'You get the drink. I'll see to the fire.'

As she handed him a glass of whisky, the remains of a bottle her father had left, their eyes met.

'Vanessa, I came to apologise. I realised too late that I had been insensitive and rude. I do owe you an explanation for the incident in the boat and I think then that you may understand.'

She sat down on the sofa and he took the chair opposite but his eyes never left her.

'Four years ago my wife and son were

drowned while out fishing.' He stopped and searched her face for a reaction as flames leapt round the logs and cast flickering shadows across his face adding to the shadows of sorrow which were already there.

When she didn't speak he continued, 'It was a day similar to Friday. Helen loved fishing and she would take Joe with her whenever she could. I should have warned her about the weather but I had no idea she had planned on going fishing after such a foul night.'

He paused, struggling with his emotions. 'By morning it had brightened and I was working out on the hills with Angus bringing the sheep down. But she knew the signs, which is why I've never understood what made her go. The squalling rain came up quickly and we eventually had to take shelter and then abandon work altogether.'

His face was contorted with pain and she tried to stop him, to tell him not to dig up the past but he needed to go on. 'They found the bodies three days later and the boat broken up on the rocks. I've never been able to talk about it since. I don't know why I'm telling you except that when I saw you on Friday in the dinghy I just knew I had to get you ashore and safe. I couldn't go through it all again.'

His eyes were holding hers, the pain replaced with something she couldn't quite fathom and the fear in her stomach gripped tight.

'I'm sorry,' she said. It was as if telling the story had released a tension in him and suddenly he became much more light hearted.

'You're a lousy sailor, but from what I hear you're not a bad teacher. Hettie thinks very highly of you.'

'Yes, well, that's all finished now, isn't it?'

'No, not necessarily. In fact part of my plan in coming here this evening was to try to persuade you to stay on a little longer, that is if you don't have anything particularly pressing to return to the prosperous south for.'

She laughed with relief at his change of mood and was uplifted by the tender play of a smile round his mouth. He wanted her to stay. It didn't matter why or what for. She had not been dismissed after all.

'Hettie and I were wondering if you would work with the children on some drama and art work. You could live in the cottage rent-free and we could arrange a small salary. What do you say?'

'As a matter of fact I have a plan of my own which I wanted to tell you about.' His face registered interest. 'I've felt since I've been here the lack of any form of entertainment on the island, both for the islanders and the visitors.'

'Visitors don't come here for entertainment,' he said shortly.

She was surprised at his abrupt reaction. 'Surely more would come if there was some, and that in return would be good for the island.'

'No, it wouldn't be right.'

'Why not? You haven't even heard

what I've got in mind yet.'

'Go on, tell me.'

'A group performing plays on all the islands, a touring company.'

His face was hard. 'And I suppose your old cronies from The Hole would form part of this group. Glamorous Greg and flirtatious Felicity.'

She was annoyed at this criticism of her friends and wasn't prepared to allay his fears by telling him Greg had no intention of being any part of it.

'Yes, that's right they would.'

He smiled cynically and shook his head. 'No, the answer's no.'

She flared at this. 'What do you mean, the answer's no? I wasn't asking your permission. I was simply telling you of my plans. I thought you might be interested. But you're so self-opinionated. You take it upon yourself to see to everything on the island; you have your finger in everything. Everyone thinks you're wonderful and you lap it up, don't you? You behave as if you owned the island.' She was pink with exertion, on her feet now and storming down at him.

His expression hardened, the smile fading at her onslaught. Then he rose and looked down at her and with cold clarity said, 'As a matter of fact, I do.'

She was stopped in her tracks. 'You do, what?'

'I do own the island. I buried my father two weeks ago which was why I had to return so hurriedly. Now I take over his estate and this small island just happens to be part of it. A very small part of it, but the part I hold most dearly, and I will not allow a tin pot theatre company to turn it into a second rate holiday resort.' He picked up his jacket and walked out into the night leaving her dumb and staring after him.

* * *

Why on earth had he told her that? She made him open up and tell her things he never discussed with anyone. How he wished she would go home with her friends and leave him in peace. He should never have listened to Hettie with her ideas about Vanessa helping out at the school. The children had a teacher now. They didn't need her. He would not allow these strange theatre folk loose on his island. It was his sanctuary, the only place he felt at home.

Her first reaction as she stood at the open door was one of sheer disbelief. Part of her wanted to run after the disappearing figure as it trekked down the rough road and then dipped over the cliff to take the short cut back to Fisherman's Cottage.

He owned the island. He owned a huge estate. He wasn't the man she had thought he was, someone just like herself struggling to make sense of life. He was a powerful and wealthy man, and yet he had singled her out among all the visitors to his island and spent time with her.

Just an hour ago she had been so close to him for that brief time while he had told her of his feelings and sorrows and she had almost seen behind the depths of those dark eyes. Four years had passed since the tragedy and yet he still lived it every day of his life.

Despite her concern for Robert's past traumas, anger was growing within her as his high handed attitude, both to her and to the island people.

He may own the island but he did not own the people and he had no right to decide what was right for them and what was not. And he did not have a divine right over her movements either. The people must decide and if they wanted entertainment, she would make sure they had it.

She saw her friends off in the fishing boat with Robert on Wednesday morning.

Greg held her close and it brought back so many warm feelings of love. Then they stood holding hands and looking into each other's eyes until she couldn't bare the sadness and hurt any longer and the tears began to roll down her cheeks. He didn't say anything, just squeezed her hands and turned away.

Denise hugged her. 'Don't worry, love. Be strong. We'll be back soon.'

Robert was impatient to get away and almost hustled them on board.

When they became a dot on the horizon she wandered aimlessly along the quay reluctant to return to her empty cottage so walked slowly up the hill towards the school.

Hettie was delighted to see her in the school-house which adjoined the school itself. It was a cosy, thick walled, stone building with an excess of old but comfortable furniture.

'My mother was teacher here before me, and she was the first. Before that the little ones had lessons in church from the minister.

'Well, dear, it is nice to see you.' Hettie winked at her conspiratorially. 'I see you didn't go back with your friends then.'

There was a shriek from the school-room next door and a crash followed by the sound of a child crying. Vanessa jumped up but Hettie beckoned her to sit again.

'Take no notice, Vanessa, it's only our new school teacher taking lessons. Goodness knows how she ever became a teacher for she cannot manage the children. They run rings round her and have a fine old time. I don't know why I ever worried about them. They are more than capable of looking after themselves in my absence.'

'But that was crying I heard. Surely one of them must be hurt.'

'I doubt it. It's wee Jamie. I can tell his cry anywhere. And the sound he's making now is not crying. He's maybe having our nice new school teacher on a bit.'

Vanessa laughed. Jamie would surely triumph over any adversity.

'Now what was it you came for?' Hettie asked. 'Are you going to take up my suggestion and spend a wee bit of time helping out?'

'Hettie, I've come to ask you about something. It's very important that you give me your honest opinion.'

'Now, would I do anything else?'

Looking at the warm sincerity in her face Vanessa felt confident.

'Would the islanders enjoy some entertainment? Would it go down well with the visitors, attract more to the island, maybe?'

Hettie looked at her, puzzled. 'You mean music and dancing, a sort of seaside show you get at the end of the pier?'

Vanessa laughed at the idea. 'No, I mean plays.'

'Of course, you're an actress,' Hettie interrupted and a light came into her face. 'A repertory theatre, here on the island.' She was thoughtful. 'A permanent theatre here, it would be wonderful.' She looked hard at Vanessa. 'You couldn't do it, dear. Financially it wouldn't pay. You'd never get professionals living on this island and working for peanuts.'

Vanessa continued enthusiastically. 'No, not a permanent theatre on the island. I mean travelling from place to place, performing in the ceilidh hall, say bringing a different play here about six times a year, something like that. And I've already got three of my friends interested.' She frowned. 'Finances are the problem, I admit. But, if we could get a grant to get started, do you think it would go down well?'

Hettie was definite. 'Yes, I do, if you put on the right sort of plays. We're a fairly quiet people with cultured tastes and a feeling for tradition, but we like to laugh, too. You'd have to gauge your audience.'

'Yes, I realise that.'

'Have a go, then, dear, and I'll do anything I can to help you.'

Vanessa was so happy she almost forgot to mention her other intention. 'And of course I'll plan some work-shops during the afternoons of our visits for the children. Maybe we can work with them and put on a children's show as well. It's very exciting.' Then a cloud crossed her face.

'What is it?' Hettie asked.

'Robert's not keen on the idea and I

think he'll try to stop me. I didn't realise he owned the island. Does he really have that much power?'

Hettie looked at her sympathetically. 'He's a good man, Vanessa. His father owned a large estate and was a typical laird who used the crofters to swell his own coffers. His great grandfather cleared a whole area of crofts on this island once to build his own holiday home. It's the house Janice and Steven are turning into a hotel.

'Robert's been good to the islanders and fought for them on many occasions against his father. In fact I think we've been left alone recently just to keep the peace, and there has been some investment. Things are different now, the crofters do have rights, but they all respect Robert and seem content with their lot so I don't think they would ever go against his wishes.'

Vanessa knew she was probably right.

'Had his father been ill for long?' she asked.

'Yes, we've all been waiting to hear of

his death for years. He's suffered a series of strokes and became progressively more incapacitated, but he wouldn't hand over the reins to Robert.'

'But why didn't you tell me all this before? I didn't know who Robert was or that his father was ill and had died. Why all the secrecy?'

'It's the way Robert wanted it, dear. He asked us all to respect his privacy when he first came to live here. He wanted to just be one of the islanders. So we went along with it. He and Helen were like any other family and we all loved them and their wee bairn. We are all fiercely loyal to him and would never let him down. When we heard of his father's death last week it was hardly a shock. Hardly caused a comment in fact.'

Then she smiled encouragement. 'I think it's a very good idea, though, your theatre. There are plenty of other islands. And once you're established, who knows? Maybe our Robert will come round to the idea.'

'Oh, Hettie, I hope so. At least I can spend some time with the children before I leave.'

'That would be grand,' Hettie said. 'Now let's have a nice cup of tea and you can tell me more of your plans. Oh, I'm so glad you've decided to stay on for a while.'

★　★　★

Vanessa spent a lot of time during the next couple of days talking to the islanders to try to establish what sort of plays they would enjoy and what their reactions to her plans were. Even if she never got her group to the island, it would give her some sort of feedback.

The children were in no doubt about what they wanted.

'Could we not have a pantomime?' Emma asked timidly. 'My mummy took me to see one in Edinburgh once when we went to visit my aunt.'

The reaction from Janice was disheartening. 'You'll never do it. Give up now before you wear yourself out with frustration. If the McKenzies decide you don't bring a show to the island, then you don't. It's that simple.'

Vanessa strode back to her cottage undeterred. She had spent two days now and had planned every step out on paper from approaching the appropriate Arts Council, advertising for actors and gathering support.

She knew exactly what she wanted to do and had every intention of carrying it through, confident that Robert would eventually see sense as everyone she had talked to on the island wanted her to succeed.

When she opened the door, a scrap of paper on the hall mat caught her eye. It was in scrawled writing and read: *Please call at boatyard. Urgent Message.*

A feeling of panic seized her and she hoped it was not bad news. Rushing down to the quay she looked around for Angus imagining the message had been left by him, as he seemed to attend to most things in Robert's absence.

He was nowhere to be found among the boats and she hurriedly looked in at the small office where ferry times were displayed and notices posted, but found that empty.

As a last resort she popped her head in at the tearoom where several climbers were having refreshments before returning to their cottages after a morning up in the mountains. Morag was hurrying around serving and didn't see her immediately, so Vanessa had to catch her as she passed with a tray of dishes.

'Ah, there you are, Vanessa. Angus has been looking for you. Have you not seen him yet?'

'No, but I did get a message to come down here.'

'Yes, now I believe you've to go over to Mallaig on the motor launch with him this afternoon. So you'd best be here by two-thirty.'

'What for?' Vanessa asked in alarm.

Morag smiled reassuringly. 'I'm sure

there's nothing to worry about but I should take your belongings just in case. Robert wasn't very clear as to why he wanted you so urgently.'

Vanessa was in a state of nerves for the next two hours while she packed her case and cleaned and tidied the cottage.

Could one of her parents be ill? She'd had a letter from them yesterday saying they were both fine, and full of encouragement for her new venture. She phoned them but there was no reply. Then there was a knock at the door and Maude bustled in without waiting to be invited.

'So you're off then and I suppose you'll be travelling back home now.'

Maude seated herself on the edge of one of the dining chairs and stared hard at Vanessa.

'What's this all about?' Vanessa was nonplussed.

'Now, I'm the last one to know what his lordship is about, but you'd be best to take heed. If he doesn't want you here, then you'd best be going.'

Vanessa's uneasiness was turning to anger.

'And what business is it of yours?' she snapped, unable to control her growing dislike for this woman.

Maude bristled and stuck her hands deeper into her apron pockets. 'Don't you get shirty with me, miss. You're not welcome here. You came on holiday and now your holiday is up. So if I were you I'd go along home and not outstay your welcome. Go and catch your man back where you belong and leave our Robert alone.'

It was the first real hostility Vanessa had experienced from the island people and this direct reference to her associating with Robert touched a raw nerve and put her on the defensive.

'Look, I'm sorry about what happened to your daughter. But I'm not trying to catch Robert, whatever you think — ' She was going to continue and try to explain about her plans for the theatre but the bitter fury welling in

Maude's face forced her words to trail away.

'You know nothing,' Maude hissed. 'Nothing at all. You come here with your fancy ideas and your fancy clothes.' Her arms jerked at Vanessa alarmingly.

Then she became still, her eyes darkened and there was menace in her voice. 'We've suffered on this island. You know nothing of our suffering. And now there is a price to be paid. And that price will be paid.'

Vanessa backed away from the sinister words and Maude gave her a long penetrating look then turned and left, and Vanessa found it difficult to control her trembling body.

Could this really just be a trick to get her off the island and out of harm's way? Yet she couldn't overlook the possibility that there was a real emergency which had nothing at all to do with Maude, and that the woman was just venting her spite before Vanessa left. There was no time for further pondering. She had to go and find out what it was all about. It was nearly two o'clock so she shut the cottage door and humped her bag down to the quay.

Vanessa Meets Robert's Family

The motor launch was as luxurious inside as out and Angus handled it expertly. She stood on deck as he manoeuvred the craft out of the harbour and into the open sea. Realising she was alone on the boat increased her anxiety more. Whatever the reason, Robert had arranged for her to return to the mainland in his own private boat.

'Do you know what's happened?' she asked Angus. He stared ahead and clutched the wheel, turning small amounts all the time to maintain a steady course.

'What Robert does is his own business. He doesnae confide in me, lassie.' Standing there with dark tough skin, bushy beard and knot-like muscles the Scot was a man of few words.

Vanessa sighed and lapsed into

thought as the boat bounced against the oncoming waves and a light spray splashed her face.

As land appeared Vanessa was amazed at how quickly the trip could be done in a fast boat.

'You'd think Robert would use this boat all the time instead of his old fishing boat. It's so much faster.'

'That's not his way. He's not one for speed is our Robert. He bought this boat for emergencies only. It's always moored in the bay in case the need arises.'

This increased Vanessa's anxiety once again. What emergency had incurred its use on this occasion? Her heart began to pump and she paced the deck to try to calm her nerves.

'Now just calm yourself, we're here now. You'll soon find what it's all about.'

'But where am I supposed to go when I get ashore?'

'Do not fret, lass. I'll not leave you stranded,' he reassured her.

As Angus motored in through the moored yachts and larger fishing boats several were landing their catch, tying up and putting their nets to dry. The sun was still high in the sky even though it was late afternoon, and its warmth could be felt now that they were sheltered from the fresh sea breeze.

Angus secured the boat and then put a plank across for her to walk ashore. He looked round the quay and then took her arm and propelled her towards a waiting car with a uniformed chauffeur standing beside it.

'Why now, there's James to meet you.' The two men exchanged a few words and Vanessa was helped into the back of the large saloon car. She was so surprised that it took her several minutes to even ask where she was being taken.

'Kilmorgan, Ma'am,' the chauffeur said in a clipped voice. 'Mr McKenzie is waiting for you there. It's about an hour's drive.'

Vanessa watched the uncommunicative face and realised she was wasting her time making any more inquiries. At least in an hour's time she would be able to ask Robert what it was all about. She sank back in the comfortable leather seat and felt an unexpected tingle of excitement at the thought of seeing him again.

'Just ahead, Ma'am,' the chauffeur volunteered later. 'You can just see the north tower now. Most of the castle is hidden behind the trees.'

Vanessa stared as the grey stone emerged against the sky. 'The castle?' she questioned.

'Yes, that's Kilmorgan Castle. Been the home of the McKenzies for three centuries. One of the finest castles in Scotland.'

★　★　★

Robert waited anxiously, watching for the car to draw up outside the window. Would she come? It had been a crazy

194

idea, dragging her all the way from the island on a whim.

The grey stone building emerged slowly from behind the trees as the car wound up the curved drive and Vanessa's heart beat faster as the reality of the situation dawned.

A butler in uniform opened the door and she was led through a lofty hall with a magnificent sweeping staircase and into the library where comfortable leather settees and chairs were placed round a low table. There was an enormous stone fireplace and the walls were lined from top to bottom with shelves of leather bound volumes.

When Robert walked into the room dressed in casual cream trousers and woven shirt he seemed out of place and she couldn't reconcile him with this stately home.

She jumped up and went to him anxiously. 'What's happened?'

He smiled at her, a look of surprise in his expression. 'Nothing. Why?'

Vanessa frowned. 'Why did you bring

me here? I thought maybe my parents were ill.'

He shook his head. 'No, no, I just brought you over for dinner. I thought you'd enjoy a change now that your family and friends have gone home.'

Her immediate feeling of relief quickly turned to incredulity. 'You mean you dragged me off the island like that, at a moment's notice, just to give me dinner!'

He raised his eyebrows. 'Did you have a more pressing engagement?'

The note of sarcasm in his voice inflamed her to anger. 'You know very well I didn't. But did it occur to you that I may just have been enjoying the peace and quiet? That was the reason I went to the island in the first place.'

'Oh, I thought you were just filling in time between jobs,' he drawled, still teasing.

'You had no right to assume I wanted to have dinner with you?'

'And don't you?'

The direct look in this now familiar

eyes softened her and she shook her head in defeat.

'Yes, I suppose I do. Only you needn't have frightened me to death. Why couldn't you have asked me properly?'

'You may have refused,' he said simply.

She had to grin, and the relief showed as he took her hand and kissed her lightly. 'I'll make sure you're glad you came,' he promised.

'Bridget will show you to your room and then when you're ready you can come and meet my mother. Dinner isn't until eight tonight. My uncle and aunt are coming over, too. It was one of the reasons I wanted you here so badly, a bit of moral support, you know. They won't harp on about my shortcomings with you here.'

She looked at him questioningly. 'Are you sure I'm not intruding on a family gathering; with your father having just died?'

'My father's been ill for years so my

mother was expecting it. I've never got along with him anyway and we're not exactly a close family. His brother, the uncle who's coming this evening, hasn't spoken to him for five years, but he's fond of my mother so it's all a bit of a relief really.'

The room she was shown to by the housekeeper was large and airy with a huge window overlooking the formal gardens and in the distance, towering mountains, dark now against the blazing sky.

She changed quickly, glad of the dress Robert had bought for her for the party and almost immediately there was a knock on her bedroom door. When she opened it, a tall young woman with a serious but kindly face smiled at her. She was plainly dressed and Vanessa immediately felt uncomfortably out of place.

'Hello, Vanessa, I'm Alice, Robert's sister, and I've been sent to bring you down for dinner. The family is already having drinks and they're anxious to meet you. Are you ready for the ordeal?'

Vanessa shivered with apprehension. 'Yes, I think so.'

It was a very grand room and they were seated each side of a low table in front of a crackling fire in a huge marble fireplace. The men were formally dressed and rose as she entered, Robert giving her an appreciative smile.

'He began the introductions then, turning to a pretty red-haired girl, he pulled her playfully in front of him. 'You've met my quiet sister, now this is Marie, the noisy one,' he teased.

Then he turned to a homely looking woman with a fresh complexion and dark greying hair. 'And this is my mother.'

Mary McKenzie took Vanessa's hand and drew her into the circle. 'Why, you're shivering, my dear. Robert, fetch my fur wrap for Vanessa. The poor girl isn't used to our draughty old castle.'

Robert gave Vanessa a knowing smile and went on his errand.

Then everyone was talking to her at once.

Marie perched beside her on the arm of the chair. She was slim with a freckled face and dreamy eyes. 'Oh, Vanessa, I love your dress. I should so love to shop in London. You are so lucky. I wish I could go to the theatre and see you acting. It is so glamorous to be an actress. What are you to be in next?'

It all came out in such a rush of excitement that Vanessa didn't quite know where to start answering her.

'Hold on, lass,' Uncle Jim said. 'Let Vanessa get her breath. I expect you get tired of people asking you the same questions.'

'But are you really famous?' Marie persisted. 'I saw Macbeth when I was at school. It was wonderful.'

'Our company was thinking of The Tempest next,' Vanessa said, trying to keep up with the conversation and feeling she should say something.

But Marie was unstoppable. 'Wasn't that about an island and an evil monster called Caliban? Yes and the main character was Prospero and he was very powerful.

But he relinquished his power over the island eventually, didn't he?' Marie pondered.

'He did, but through strength, not weakness.' Robert's voice was very controlled. He had entered the room with the fur and was now standing just behind her.

Vanessa froze. She hadn't connected the play with Robert's situation.

He gently placed the fur round her shoulders, letting his fingers drift across the nape of her neck, sending shivers down her spine.

An uncomfortable silence fell in the room and his mother was left to rescue the situation. 'I think we are ready to eat now.'

Robert took her arm and steered her through the long chilly corridors to another stately room where a magnificent chandelier illuminated a long table set with silver and sparkling glasses. Vanessa wished she were back in her cottage and not having to cope with all this.

As soon as the meal could be politely concluded Robert excused himself and took Vanessa's hand. 'Come on, I'll show you round. Fortunately we do have electricity here,' he laughed, as he steered her along corridors and through lofty arched rooms with exquisitely painted ceilings.

He explained the history of every picture and tapestry, told her which notable people had slept in the four-poster beds and explained how uncomfortable the horse hair mattresses were. Crumbling stone steps led up to a bell tower and turret hideaways.

'I used to daydream here as a child,' he told her on one of the battlements as they stood looking down at the loch. The sun had dropped behind the mountain now and the sky was a crimson blaze, the water of the loch a still pool of liquid gold.

Their eyes met and his hand touched hers tentatively at first and then took hold. His deep dark eyes held her, his face shadowy in the fading light.

He had removed his jacket and tie after dinner and rolled up the sleeves of his crisp white shirt so that the hairs on his chest and arms showed against his weather-darkened skin, his muscles strong and firm. Yet his hand gripping hers was soft and gentle.

'I'm glad you're here,' he said. 'I've missed you.'

'Me, too,' she whispered.

She knew he was going to kiss her and the anticipation was glorious. He moved closed and she felt the touch of his other hand on her cheek and then he softly brushed aside her thick dark hair and slipped his hand round her head to draw her to him, his lips touching her lightly at first and then with sensuous eagerness.

Then he drew back and something in his expression told her he had remembered and the memory still hurt and Vanessa wasn't part of it.

She swallowed and turned away.

Almost immediately he recovered and slipped his arm round her waist.

'Come on, we'll walk down to the loch.'

There was still a warm companionship between them. Standing on the bank looking into the still dark water, he leant his cheek against her hair. 'I wish I could forget,' he said almost to himself.

'I don't think you ever will, but it must get easier as time goes by.'

'Not the guilt, that will never leave me. It was my fault, you see.'

'What do you mean?' Vanessa asked nervously.

He seemed in a dream, not talking to her at all. 'It was the storm, I suppose. But they may have stood a chance if . . . I just didn't expect them to go out that morning. The storm was raging all night.

'I taught her to fish, and Joe. They both loved it. It's not a woman's job, yet Helen was a natural. I shouldn't have taught her. She didn't know the coast like me. She couldn't judge the weather. I should never have let her fish alone with Joe.' His face was covered with beads of perspiration and his hands formed fists at his side as he stared ahead out over the lock.

Vanessa sensed she had to tread carefully or he would clam up again and he needed to talk.

Gently she said, 'You can't blame yourself just because you taught her to fish, and how could you have stopped her from going when you didn't know her plans.'

He turned, a hard angry stare, a confusion of emotions. 'You don't know anything about it. You don't understand. I'm guilty. I've got to live with it always. There are things nobody can ever understand. Things between Helen and me. I don't want to talk about it anymore.'

Vanessa felt inadequate as if anything she could say would seem futile against the weight of his emotions. Eventually she put her hand on his arm in a gesture of comfort but he pulled away.

Then he looked at her, a haunted look in his eyes.

She shrank from the rebuff. Quickly he recovered his composure.

'I'm sorry, I shouldn't have told you all that. In fact I shouldn't have asked you here at all. I'm sorry, Vanessa.'

They continued to walk round the loch in silence, one which was heavy with words unsaid. She desperately wanted to sooth his fears, comfort him. Yet she was afraid to unleash in him emotions which she couldn't deal with.

It was almost dark when they entered the hall again and voices from the drawing room told them the family was still deep in conversation.

'I think I'll just go up to bed,' she said and he nodded, understanding her reluctance to intrude further.

As she stared to climb the stairs he called to her softly and she turned. His face was resigned but gentle. 'I'm sorry.'

She swallowed, trying to contain the awful feeling of hurt she was experiencing.

Lying in the darkness she went over

and over what he had told her. It didn't make sense. Why did she fell so guilty? There had to be more, a lot more.

Vanessa sank into the big soft bed but sleep eluded her. Somewhere in this huge castle Robert slept. She didn't know where or if he was sleeping or pacing the room in his anxiety.

Eventually she must have fallen asleep because she was woken by knocking at her bedroom door, and before she had time to answer Marie came in with a tray.

'Vanessa, wake up. It's a lovely day and we are to go to The Games today. You must get dressed quickly. But have this first.'

Marie was fussing with her pillows and the tray in a great fluster of excitement.

Vanessa sat up against the pillows and tried to clear her head and work out where she was and what was happening.

'Marie, I can't. I have to go back today. I have things to do.'

'Why, you cannot leave Scotland without seeing The Highland Games. Robert is throwing the discus and he's taking part in some of the other events, too. There's the tug o' war and hill racing. You'll love the highland dancing. And the pipe bands march all round the village.'

'Marie, will you listen to me, please?'

The girl was silenced and gave Vanessa a worried look.

'Marie, Robert doesn't want me here. I have to go home today.'

Marie sighed. 'Robert's upset you, hasn't he? He does it all the time. He's always upsetting people with his abrupt ways. He doesn't mean it, Vanessa. He really likes you, I can tell. Please talk to him. And please, please stay.'

Marie perched on the end of the bed. 'Oh, and Mother wants you to go and see her in the drawing room after breakfast.'

Mary was reading the newspaper over by the window with a pair of spectacles half way down her nose. She looked up as Vanessa came in and beckoned her to sit beside her on the couch.

Vanessa breathed in the pure air coming up over the mountains through the open window and sighed as a heron took off from the shores of the loch and soared high above the rugged peaks.

'Spectacular,' she said at last, and Mary smiled indulgently.

'Different from what you're used to?'

Vanessa nodded. 'Robert's so lucky to have spent his life among such surroundings.'

'Maybe, but we're not here to talk about Robert. I want to hear about these plans of yours.'

Vanessa looked at her in surprise, wondering what Robert had been telling her. The grey eyes were searching hers.

'I suppose you mean about the travelling theatre.' Suddenly she didn't feel that confident any more.

'Well, Robert told me you wanted to set something of the sort up to entertain the islanders. What exactly did you have in mind?'

'It would be a group of actors producing a repertoire of plays of different types which we could perform in small halls round the many islands off the coast. We could have workshops at the schools and involve the local children. It was just an idea — ' she trailed off feeling the force of those penetrating eyes.

'Excellent!' Mary said.

Vanessa jumped with surprise. 'You think so?'

'Yes, I do. I don't know why Robert is so against it.'

'I don't think he really knows what I have in mind,' Vanessa said.

'Why didn't you explain it to him?'

'He didn't give me a chance.'

Mary tutted. 'Just like him. He can be so pig-headed at times. So like his father. That's why they were always at loggerheads. Bruce would want one thing and Robert would automatically oppose him. We had no peace at all until he decided to go over and live on the island.

'Then after that dreadful accident we hoped he would come back; that some sort of truce could be called, but it was even worse then. He wouldn't communicate with us at all and it was only as his father's health began to fail that he responded to my wishes that he should visit us.'

'What a shame,' Vanessa said.

Mary shook her head. 'The old fellow's dead now and I shouldn't speak badly of him but he made a lot of enemies with his brusque manner. It was a lonely life being married to him. I think that's why Robert's a loner, you know. He never had a normal childhood. Bruce wouldn't allow him to play with the local children or the estate workers other than to give them orders.'

Vanessa was beginning to understand why Robert had broken loose from his tyrannical father and chosen a small cottage on a peaceful island and a wife of his own choosing.

'Don't give up,' Mary admonished. 'Look, enjoy your stay here. Get to know Robert better. He's not the ogre he appears. And he will listen to you if you give him a chance.'

Vanessa smiled. She wasn't convinced. But she was tempted to stay on and enjoy the day ahead; it would give her a chance to relax and forget the myriad of conflicting emotions swirling in her brain.

★　★　★

Preparations were soon underway and Vanessa found herself helping to pack an elaborate picnic into the estate car together with rugs in case it turned cold and deckchairs, umbrellas and a selection of boots to cope with muddy fields.

Marie hugged her. 'I'm so glad you're coming and I won't let Robert upset you, I promise.'

Robert was nowhere to be seen, so she was able to plod around the wet grass with Marie, watch all the activities and enjoy the atmosphere and the friendly attention she received. When she did eventually spot Robert in the distance talking to Angus she couldn't quite believe what she saw.

'He's wearing a kilt,' she shrieked and Marie laughed.

'Of course he is. It's the McKenzie tartan. What did you expect him to wear?'

And in full highland dress he looked fantastic. She just couldn't take her eyes off him and a warm glow spread through her and a longing to be with him.

He took part in several of the events and she followed him at a discreet distance just to watch from afar. Then the highland dancing attracted her attention and she watched fascinated by the intricacy of the steps. The hill racers set off and a haunting melody drifted down from a lone piper somewhere in a distant glen.

Marie pulled at her arm. 'Come on, let's have some tea. You've spent enough time watching my brother for now. I want some of your company.'

Vanessa blushed scarlet but when she saw the look of mischief in Marie's eyes she nudged her playfully and then linked her arm as they went off to find the refreshment tent.

He was in the tent standing at the bar drinking a beer when they got there and Vanessa tried not to stare at him, concentrating instead on the wonderful array of food of which she ate hungrily. Marie was distracted by a friend she spotted so left Vanessa on her own. Almost immediately Robert was by her side.

'You're still here then,' he said quietly.

His hair was still wet with perspiration and she could feel the heat from his body, his eyes telling her that he remembered yesterday and she knew their relationship had deepened.

But today demanded a light-hearted approach so she smiled, 'You did bring me here, remember?'

He gave a short laugh. 'I'm sorry. I didn't mean to be rude. I just thought you might have had enough of me and taken off back down to your friends.'

'No, I have no plans for taking off just yet,' she said firmly.

He raised his eyebrows and looked at her. 'Good, I'll be able to show you a little more of my native land then.'

In the crowded tent his body moved nearer to hers and his hand touched her arm, just the gentlest of touches, but electrifying. His voice dropped to a whisper.

'I'm sorry about today. It's all part of the tradition. I have to play my part. But tomorrow will be ours, I promise you.'

'I'm enjoying today,' she insisted. 'I like your family. I love your country. And I'm content just being here with you. You don't have to apologise.'

'But we will have tomorrow,' he insisted, squeezing her arm more urgently.

She looked up into the depths of his

troubled face. 'Of course we do.' And a wave of relief passed over his features with the beginning of a smile at the corners of his eyes.

The finale to the day was a parade of pipe and drum bands as they marched round the field, their haunting music echoing through the hillside.

Back at the castle, preparations were under way for a party to end the day. She had only enough time to freshen up and put on an extra jumper when Marie was dragging her out to join the merriment.

Though she was never left alone, Robert did not come near her. She noticed how he circulated among the estate workers and the wealthy landowners who had travelled from remote areas for the games.

A band had been hired for the evening and when the dancing began in one of the marquees Vanessa felt a surge of anticipation. Yet Robert danced only with the village girls, swirling them in turn down sets formed by the increasingly noisy gathering.

As midnight approached she made her excuses to Marie that she was about to leave and go to bed.

Walking dejectedly across the field towards the path leading up to the castle she heard someone behind her and a hand gripped her arm and swung her round.

Robert's face was close to hers and in the moonlight seemed strung with emotion. There were no words as his mouth closed over hers and he drew her so close she felt the breath being squeezed from her body. After wonderful moments he relaxed, still holding her in his arms, his face close, his eyes looking deep into hers.

Then he smiled. 'Just to let you know I hadn't forgotten you.'

She was so surprised she couldn't think of anything to say.

He smoothed her hair with his hand, hugged her close and whispered in her ear. 'Tonight I have to be sociable, but remember that tomorrow is ours.'

Then he let her go and, without a lingering look, backed away towards the marquee and the noisy music. She watched him go and smiled, her heart full of love.

'You've Become Just Like Your Father'

When Robert appeared next morning he was dressed casually and they drove out over the moorlands until they reached a remote spot where he parked the car. They began a steady climb up one of the craggy mountains and it wasn't long before Vanessa was forced to stop for breath. Wearing a tough pair of walking boots that his mother had found for her, she was much more comfortable and beginning almost to feel at home in the rugged terrain. But she could not match Robert's fitness.

She leant back against a large boulder to get her breath back and he paused beside her, studying her heaving breathlessness with amusement. Then he slipped his arm comfortably round her shoulder and began to point out various landmarks in the panorama of peaks and still, deep lochs.

'How could you bear to leave all this?' she asked.

He looked at her with sadness in his eyes. 'It wasn't by choice. I just couldn't stay any longer. My father and I argued so much it was making life intolerable for mother and the two girls.'

He continued to stare out at the distant hills, his arm firmly holding her. 'He sent me off to agricultural college to learn how to manage the estate properly, but when I came back with new and modern methods he wouldn't listen. He ran things in the same way as my grandfather and great grandfather. Nothing ever changed. The crofters got poor while he got richer.

'We all used to go to the island every year for a holiday and that year when I was twenty-two I saw things differently. Most of the islanders just rake a living from their piece of land and a few sheep. My father could have helped them, he had the money. But all he wanted to do was make more. They weren't people to him. His most recent ideas was to try to increase the use of the island for tourism, build a marina and hotel.'

She was beginning to see how old resentments were surfacing and why he was so against her plans.

'But surely that would have been good for the people by increasing their revenue and creating jobs,' she ventured.

He shook his head. 'No, it would have destroyed its peace and beauty. It would have become a playground for the rich.' He looked directly at her. 'Vanessa, I won't have that happen to the island. I fought hard to prevent him from spoiling it and I won't let anyone else.'

She held his look, then eventually he turned away. 'In the end it was resolved. He agreed to let me manage the island my own way so long as I stayed there and kept out of his life. So I settled in Fisherman's cottage and married Helen.'

'And now you can do exactly what you want with all of it,' she said viewing the endless miles of bleak forbidding land.

'Yes, but it will take time. It's my responsibility to see that things are now done the way I want them doing.'

She was conscious of his closeness, the warmth of his arm on her shoulder. Nothing must spoil the moment. They continued their climb, more slowly now, as if the weight of responsibility was holding him back.

'I'd like to return to the island tomorrow, Robert. I've enjoyed the break, but I do have unfinished business there,' she said.

'What business?' he enquired sharply, his mood changed

'Well, for one thing, I promised Hettie I'd do some work with the children, produce another concert.'

'Yes, and what is the second thing?'

'I have letters to write and I'm expecting some mail at the cottage.'

'You're still intent on this seaside

show idea, aren't you? It may be suitable for Brighton, but not for the island.'

She turned on him. 'It is not going to be a seaside show. Why are you determined to think the worst of me? What I have in mind is a selection of plays of different types, some very serious.'

He gave a hard laugh. 'Serious! What, with your friend, Felicity, and that great gawking blond boy. Don't make me laugh.'

His sarcasm inflamed her anger. 'Felicity may be glamorous and out-going but she is professional and very serious about her career. Greg is an extrovert, yes, but he's a brilliant actor.'

'I'm sure they are all very talented but they do not fit in on the island.'

'Anyway, Greg isn't even interested in my project,' Vanessa retorted.

Robert's eyebrows rose. 'So, the love of your life is deserting, is he?'

Vanessa was finding his taunting increasingly difficult to contend with.

'Oh, Greg and I understand each other. We've worked together for a long time and we respect each other,' she said, trying to put Robert down.

But it seemed only to increase his opposition. 'Then I suggest you follow his example and go back where you belong. I'm sure your talents would be wasted up here.'

The cold-disdain in his eyes stung more than the words. Surely if he cared at all he would encourage her with her plans and want to keep her here.

'I'll ask Thomas to make sure the car is ready for you in the morning.'

He really did think he could just push her off home.

'You seem to forget I rented the cottage until the end of the month,' she said.

He shrugged. 'I can arrange a refund.'

'But I don't want a refund. I want to continue my holiday until I'm ready to go home,' she shouted. But he was already walking ahead of her down the path back towards the castle.

* * *

Mary seemed surprised when Vanessa came down next morning with her bag packed. 'I'm sorry you've abandoned your ideas for the island's entertainment,' she said. 'But I suppose it wasn't a very practical proposition.'

They hugged and said their goodbyes, not needing any further explanations. Robert saw her into the car and their eyes met but they only exchanged the normal formalities.

As the car turned the bend of the road and slid behind the trees Vanessa had a last glimpse of him standing casually dressed in slacks and shirt, his emotions held too firmly in control to even allow a smile.

* * *

'Thomas, take me to Mallaig, please.' They had been driving for half an hour and her despondency was turning to anger.

'But Robert told me to take you to Glasgow. You can get a train from there.'

'Thomas, I do not wish to go to Glasgow, so please do as I ask. Just drive me to Mallaig and drop me off at a hotel there.'

'As you wish, Ma'am.'

She signed in at the hotel and ordered a coffee. At least it would give her space to think. Cradling her hands round the cup she felt her whole body slump.

Was she doing the right thing in letting Robert bully her into giving up her plans? Yet, did she really want to stay up here if he wanted nothing to do with her, thought nothing of her? It was all such a muddle.

'I won't go,' she said out loud and caused a few surprised stares in the hotel lobby.

Having made this sudden decision she felt immediately better. Humping her bag out once again, she hailed a taxi and told the driver to take her to the harbour. She was going back to the island whether Robert liked it or not.

She found a ferry that was stopping at the island after calling at several others and booked her fare. But after many hours on a choppy sea and feeling anything but well, she found that when the boat tied up alongside the jetty she was not allowed to disembark.

Angus stood at the foot of the gangway and argued vigorously with the boatman. The boatman came back on board and told Vanessa that she could not go on to the island.

'Why not?' she yelled at the boatman.

'Look, madam, I don't know all the whys and wherefores,' he said, angry at the unpleasantness. 'But if you'll just sit down and let me get off; I've a schedule to keep.'

Vanessa watched as the gap between the boat and the jetty widened and shook her head in dismay, then sank listlessly on to the wooden seat at the side of the boat and watched her island become a smaller and smaller speck in the sunset. She would go back to the hotel tonight and then set off on her journey home tomorrow. She had no more fight left in her.

* * *

'You did what?' Mary McKenzie looked up from the morning paper she was reading and let her spectacles drop on her nose.

Robert stood just inside the drawing-room door with a bundle of mail in his hand which he had brought in for his mother. 'I told Angus he must stop her returning to the island.' His expression was unfathomable.

Mary was on her feet. 'You can't do that. You have no right to.'

'I do not want those people on the island. I will do anything I can to stop them.'

'But, Robert, for goodness sake, think what you are doing. Vanessa has a strong personality. If she wants to go ahead with her plans, she will do it, you mark my words.'

'She doesn't know what she's doing. It would never work. The island's too small to support it.'

'Well, then, invest some money into it. You have the power now.'

'I intend to do that, but for the right reasons, not this theatre thing. What sort of rubbish are they going to put on?'

Mary was angry. 'Robert, Vanessa is a lovely girl. Do you really think she would associate herself with rubbish? From what I hear, it will be quality stuff. They're professionals. You're being totally irrational. I think all this power has gone to your head. You've become just like your father and I don't like what I see. Have you really talked to her about it?'

Robert visibly slumped. 'No, I suppose I haven't.'

Mary walking over to him and looked him straight in the eye. 'Do you want her to go?'

His face was contorted with pain. 'No, you know I don't.'

'Well, stop acting like your father and talk to her.'

He sighed. 'I know; but I am like my father, aren't I?'

'For goodness sake, Robert, you don't have to be. Be your own man and deal with it.'

★ ★ ★

Falling onto the bed completely exhausted, Vanessa viewed the depressingly unimaginative room. A tight-faced lady with a bun had handed her the key and a small boy in an oversized uniform carried her bag up the stairs. And now, surrounded by dismal and browning wallpaper, she felt more depressed than ever.

Reading the hotel information she saw that dinner was at six-thirty and, as it was now eight o'clock, it was useless to expect food here tonight, unless by some luck they could produce a sandwich and coffee. She really didn't feel like venturing out again.

As she pulled open the door to investigate the possibility, a figure came hurtling along the corridor and almost pushed her back into the room. Recovering her balance she found herself held in strong arms.

'What are you doing here?' she hissed at him.

Robert's face was placid, almost amused. 'I came to take you out to dinner. After the day you've had I reckoned you'd need feeding and this hotel is not your style.'

She stared at him and the situation would have made her laugh had she not been through the trauma of a day spent on an uncomfortable ferryboat and the indignity of being refused access to the island.

Despite her annoyance and tiredness she felt a warmth at his presence and an excitement at seeing him again.

'Come on, get your coat on. It's turned a bit chilly.'

'No, I'm not hungry but I am tired and I have no wish to go out with you this evening or at any other time, thank you,' she said, determined not to give in to her feelings. 'And, anyway, how did you know I was still here?'

'I know all the ferrymen.'

When he smiled she was almost lost, his eyes creasing at the corners and meeting hers in a knowing way.

'You're mad at me, aren't you?'

'Do you expect anything else?' she retorted.

He shook his head. 'I told you, Vanessa, I don't want you interfering on my island. I have a right to prevent anyone from doing that.'

'No, I don't think you do. Times have changed and you can't stop me going on the island if I want to. You're as bad as your father. You criticised him for the way he did things and now you're doing exactly the same. You don't care about the people who live on that island, people like Hettie and Angus, you don't care that those children are growing up starved of culture, knowing nothing of the outside world until they leave and then they never go back. You don't care about — '

He gripped her shoulders and pulled her towards him so that her face was close and she could see bitterness in his eyes. 'Yes, I do care about them. I cared about them enough to stop my father and I care enough about them to stop you. It's a beautiful, peaceful island, one of the few places left where you can relax away from noisy entertainment and holiday-makers. I want none of it here. And, believe it or not, I care about you.'

His face was close now, their lips almost touching and she could see the passion in his eyes, the hungry longing in every line of his face. His hands moved from her shoulders and round her back as his lips touched hers, silencing any retort she may have made.

Vanessa felt her iron resolve weaken at the warmth of his kiss and as his hand slipped round her waist her legs turned to jelly and all her anger disappeared.

For several moments he held her, his kisses passionate, his arms strong, his body warm, and she wanted the present to last for ever.

Just as suddenly he pulled away from her and quickly recovered his enchanting smile. 'Dinner now?' he enquired, and before she knew what was happening they were on their way down the threadbare staircase.

'I'm not dressed for dinner,' she said once she'd got herself together.

'You look fine to me for the place I have in mind.'

What Robert had in mind was fish and chips eaten out of the paper sitting on an upturned lobster pot on the quay. Fishermen were cleaning their nets and tidying up boats. There were courting couples out for an evening stroll and a man walking his dog as the setting sun lit up the sky with a scarlet glow which reflected deep gold on the still water.

'Do you really want me to leave and go back home?' she asked as he sat close to her, his arm possessively round her waist.

He looked at her seriously. 'You know I don't.'

His lips brushed her hair and his

hand tightened on her waist. 'I've arranged for you to see someone tomorrow, in Inverness. Thomas will take you over in the car. It's a theatrical agency my mother knows of. I talked to them today and I think they may be able to help you.'

Vanessa listened in disbelief, not wanting to enquire further; feeling the ice she was treading was very thin. Was he really prepared to help her after all?

Hardly able to contain her happiness she turned and flung her arms round his neck and kissed him recklessly. Quickly he disentangled himself and looked quite taken aback and embarrassed. Despite this, as he held her close, his look held the warmth of love.

Robert Reveals His Tortured Soul

Vanessa was waiting in the hotel lobby when Thomas came to collect her. The journey to Inverness was comfortable and full of anticipation, the road narrow and winding, ranged on each side by towering mountains with bleak summits swathed in cloud.

Thomas was polite but uncommunicative which gave Vanessa time to ponder the events of the past twenty-four hours. She still couldn't understand Robert's about turn.

As they approached the town her excitement grew, but when Thomas stopped the car in a rather rundown area and Vanessa was directed up to the third floor of a tatty office block, doubts were beginning to surface.

'Sit in here, please,' a surly woman

barked, taking her into a glass partitioned waiting area. 'Mr Salcombe will see you in a moment.'

A young woman came in and took a seat beside Vanessa, her hair frizzed and bleached and her fingernails in need of cleaning.

'You waiting to see Mr Salcombe, too?' she enquired.

Vanessa replied curtly, not anxious to get into conversation.

'Had any work lately?' the blonde persevered.

'I'm not here looking for work,' Vanessa said.

The blonde raised her eyebrows. 'Lucky you, I haven't had anything in six months now. Nothing much going up here. Think I'll have to move down south and try me luck there. You come from down south, do you?'

Vanessa found herself being drawn into a conversation with the woman against her will and as the time passed her irritation grew.

When eventually she was shown into

Mr Salcombe's office, a tatty untidy room, full of dusty papers, half eaten sandwiches and yesterdays coffee cups, she was ready to give him a piece of her mind.

'Sit down, dearie,' he said, hustling some papers and not even bothering to look at her. 'I must have your particulars here somewhere if I can just put my hands on them.'

'What particulars?' she snapped at him.

He looked over his half height glasses and peered at her when he heard the tone of her voice.

'You did fill in a C.V. I presume.'

'C.V.? What are you talking about?'

'Well, I've got to know what you can do if I'm going to find you work, dearie?' he said in a tired voice.

'I'm not looking for work, Mr Salcombe,' she said calmly, convinced now that he had not connected her with Robert. He was not listening.

'Vanessa Sanderson, sent to me on the recommendation of Robert McKenzie with a plea to find you some acting work in the area,' he read from a scrap of paper he had found.

He put the paper down and looked up at her. 'I owe the McKenzies a favour or two. I'm sure we can find something which will suit you. But I really must know what you can do, so if you'll just fill in some details on this form and leave it with my receptionist, then I'll let you know if anything crops up. Next please.'

Vanessa was speechless. No longer was she angry with the silly little man who thought she was some third-rate actress desperate for work. That Robert could send her to this tatty, disreputable place, she just couldn't believe. In cold fury she stormed past the astonished receptionist and straight into a very tall thin young man on his way in.

She disentangled herself and apologised.

'You're in a bit of a state, aren't you?' he said in a warm, caring way.

'Yes, I am,' Vanessa agreed, smoothing herself down.

'Getting you down, is it? Not much

these days for the likes of us.'

Vanessa stared into the clean-shaven face and was calmed by the sincerity in his pale blue eyes. 'Haven't had any work this year,' he shrugged. 'All the qualifications, experience in everything I've been able to wheedle my way into, but still no work.'

Vanessa found herself studying this young man with professional interest. There was something about him, something she liked.

'Well, better go through the motions so to speak. See old Salcombe, not that he'll have anything on offer, never does. Shirley comes here regularly, too. She's brilliant on stage, scatty as they come off, but can that girl act.'

'Who's Shirley?'

'In there. Got an appointment after me. The blonde one. She said she'd been talking to you.'

'You say she can act, that she's good?'

'Good thing her old man's got money or she'd be working in a factory now and all that talent gone to waste. Anyway, must go in now. Good luck. Hope you find what you're looking for.'

Vanessa felt her spirits lifting and she put a restraining hand on the young man's arm. 'I think I just have.'

He looked at her questioningly. 'What's that?'

She smiled at him. 'I think I may have found what I'm looking for.'

'Oh, good.' Then he turned to continue on his way into the office. But Vanessa quickly placed herself in his path. 'Have you got time for a coffee somewhere?' Vanessa felt a flush of embarrassment when she realised, by the shocked look the man was giving her, what this must have seemed to him. 'I have a business proposition to put to you.'

The bell rang again and the receptionist came towards them.

'Mr Salcombe has rung for you twice, Mr Jeffrey. Would you mind going in straight away, please.'

She put on her most beguiling smile

and said, 'I think I may have some work to offer you, only I don't have a lot of time to spare.'

The young man looked at her with interest. 'Really! Well, in that case I'm all yours. Alan Jeffrey at your service, madam!' he said. Then turning to the receptionist. 'You see how it is. Opportunities like this don't arise every day.'

The woman watched as they walked to the door, her face a picture of amazed curiosity.

As they passed the glass partitioned waiting area Vanessa went over to Shirley. 'I don't want to raise your hopes or promise anything but I have an idea which may interest you. I'm just about to discuss it over coffee with Alan so maybe you would like to join us.'

Shirley dropped a nail file she'd been using into her handbag and snapped it shut. 'Well, a chance is more than he'll give me in there,' she said nodding in the direction of Mr Salcombe's office. 'A chance is all an actress can hope for these days.' With this she swaggered after them into the street.

★ ★ ★

The three complemented each other to perfection. Alan had talent, energy and enthusiasm while Shirley's family had the money, and it appeared would be prepared to use it to further her career in any possible way.

'We'll all go and talk to Dad at the weekend,' Shirley said. He lived in Bolton and had made his millions as an entrepreneur; had begun with a window cleaning round, ended up with an extensive office cleaning empire and invested heavily in the stock market.

Vanessa dismissed Thomas in Mallaig and returned to her hotel full of enthusiasm. Things were really taking off now. She didn't care whether Robert would allow her on to his precious island or not. She would contact the others and together with Alan and Shirley they would set up their company.

With the promised financial backing they could pay for publicity and survive for the months it took to work up a small repertoire of plays. Then when the bookings started to arrive they would tour the country and perform their work.

By dinnertime she was ravenous and even the rubbery steak and kidney pudding tasted palatable. She chatted amiably to the other guests and felt altogether happier than she had for months. With the excitement of her new venture she found it difficult to sleep that night, the cry of gulls round the harbour waking her at first light from a restless sleep.

There was nothing much to do now until the weekend except plan and dream. So it was a welcome intrusion when Thomas appeared mid morning at the hotel desk requesting her to accompany him to Kilmorgan Castle to have lunch with Robert and Mrs McKenzie.

She smiled and told him she would

be delighted to. Inwardly she gloated over the opportunity to tell Robert just how successful his arranged interview had been, how she had found just exactly the right work, and how helpful the agency was.

Robert was anxious. Would she come? Had he done the right thing sending her to the agency? He wanted her to stay near, couldn't bear to lose her. But these strange friends she wanted to bring along gave him nightmares. He didn't feel comfortable with them. He wanted just Vanessa. She was different. Or was she?

As she stepped out of the car at Kilmorgan Castle, Robert emerged from the estate office, a converted stable block at one side of the courtyard. His hair curled untidily over his forehead, taking the gloating feeling away from her and filling her with tenderness.

He turned and walked back into the office expecting her to follow. Rustling through some papers on his desk he spoke to her without looking up. 'I thought we could have some lunch and then take a walk up the hills round the loch. Mother enjoys your company and she doesn't see many people around here.'

Vanessa felt the excitement drain from her. 'So that's why you asked me here, to keep your mother company.'

He looked up at her with surprise. 'No, it isn't and you know it. Don't keep jumping down my throat, Vanessa. Look, I asked you here for lunch, I sent a car to pick you up, and I tried to fix you up with some work. What more can I do to show friendship?'

'Friendship!' She spat the word out and his eyes narrowed. He stood up straight and walked round to face her.

'Is that such a bad thing?'

The hurt she felt caught her by surprise; her legs were having difficulty in supporting her and she could feel her mouth begin to tremble. The only possibility of coming out of this encounter with any self respect was to try to walk out of his office without another word and find his mother. He didn't stop her but she could feel the force of his stare burning into her back.

She soon became totally lost in the conglomeration of outbuildings, many adapted for storage of heavy farm equipment and long defunct machinery.

Tears were blinding her at the frustration of her situation and this mixed with anger. Why was she here at all? What right had this man to treat her in this way, expecting her to come to him on demand, dismissing her when he pleased, dictating what she could and could not do?

She would reach the house and instruct the first person she met to order a taxi for her. And then she would drive away from this place, away from Robert McKenzie and never again would she succumb to his wishes.

Not looking where she was going in her resolve to escape, she didn't see a hosepipe coiled untidily across the yard, caught her foot and sprawled inelegantly across the concrete, grazing both knees so that blood dripped down her legs. Sitting amidst the maze of buildings, she cursed softly as she dabbed them with her handkerchief and dusted gravel off her hands. Not only was she totally lost in this monstrous place but she now looked and felt a complete wreck.

Hobbling out of the deserted yard, she wondered where all the estate workers could be. On previous visits it had seemed that there were men everywhere yet today she had not set eyes on anyone.

Determined not to endure the humiliation of returning to the office to receive one of Robert's pitying looks she stumbled on round a great tower and into a grassy courtyard with a fountain playing peacefully at its centre. Perching on its surrounding wall she dangled her feet in the pool and splashed water on to her grazed knees, immediately feeling calmer.

Why were they always at loggerheads? Why could she and Robert not quietly talk and resolve their differences? And the stark truth surfaced again and hit her squarely. Robert didn't want to. Friendship was all he could offer. And it wasn't enough. She needed his heart and his love.

She put her shoes on again, and reconciled herself to retracing her steps back to the estate office and Robert, then to her enormous relief she saw Mary bustling towards her.

Without fuss the woman guided her indoors and to the comfort of an easy chair where she cleaned her grazes and applied plasters. Then putting a glass of whisky into her hand, she positioned herself on a high-backed chair opposite to Vanessa and demanded, 'Now, I want to hear all about it. My son has been upsetting you again, I can see from your face.' She paused, her eyes full of impatient anger and not leaving Vanessa's face. 'He gets more like his father every day, I don't know why you put up with it.'

Vanessa sipped the whisky and,

feeling immediately better, she proceeded to tell Mary everything that had happened the previous day.

'You mean he sent you to that terrible man! He thought you wanted a job?'

'He said it was someone you knew.'

'Did he? Well I know him all right. He arranged some entertainment here at the castle for us once. Horrible little man.'

Eventually Robert came in and stared at the two women, a distraught expression on his face.

'Vanessa, I arranged the interview for you. Didn't that please you?'

His mother piped in. 'You should never have sent her to that awful place. Whatever possessed you?'

Robert raised his eyebrows. 'Is it awful? I thought they did a good job for you for your silver wedding celebrations.'

'Robert, you weren't even there.'

He sighed and shook his head. 'Can't I ever get anything right?'

He strode from the room and Vanessa felt a chill creep through her. Was this the end? Would she leave and never see him again?

Despite her anger she still felt impossibly attracted to him. Every movement he made sent shivers through her and his looks went straight to her heart. She had never felt like this about any man before.

'I think he was probably only trying to help,' Mary said, her mood softening. 'He does care about you, Vanessa. It was his way of trying to help, to keep you here. But as he says, he often gets it all wrong.'

Mary patted her hand. 'Don't worry too much, dear. Robert will come round eventually.'

'Please don't tell him about my plans just yet,' she said.

If he heard about how she had enlisted the help of yet another young man and another scatty blonde it would only add fuel to his arguments.

'Of course not.' She gave Vanessa a

conspiratorial wink. 'Let him stew for a bit, shall we?'

Then Robert was there again, standing just inside the door. This was it; he would ask her to leave and the stab of pain took her unawares. She had promised herself that once she left this place today, there would be no returning under any circumstances. Yet her heart craved just one more look, one touch, one kiss before saying a final goodbye.

A surge of utter relief and joy flooded through her as he stretched both hands out to her and said lightly, 'Come on, I'll take you for that walk now.'

All anger was gone with the anticipation of this last time alone with Robert.

* * *

There was a wonderful peace up amongst the heather with the clear blue sky and gentle wind. It wasn't long before his arm slipped round her waist and she felt the close warmth of his body next to hers. The necessity to talk and explain was gone and Vanessa wondered why they couldn't always feel this way. If only she could have been a simple, unambitious girl like Helen and he hadn't had an estate thrust into his keeping they could have stayed on the island and let things take their course.

'I'm sorry about yesterday,' he said quietly as they walked down a steep path to the deep dark waters of the loch. 'I wanted you to stay and I thought this was a way of doing it.'

She was silent for a moment, determined this time to set the record straight, without emotions surging out of control. 'I'm not desperate for work, Robert. My agent is always phoning with offers but I turn them down. I wanted to give the Cheltern my best shot, and now I want to do the same here. You see, I believe in small theatres. I think they're important.'

Then she turned to him, unable to maintain her aloof manner. 'I really loved the island and the people there. I care about them as much as you do. Hettie and Denise and Fiona, they are all my friends.'

'Shush,' he said quietly pulling her towards him and putting a finger over her mouth. 'I said I'm sorry. I know you're serious about this acting thing on the island and I've thought hard about it. My mother thinks it's a good idea and I value her opinion. The islanders seem to be for it.' He paused.

'Does that mean you're going to relent, not oppose me at every move?' To have Robert finally on her side was more than she had hoped for.

'Not so fast. I didn't say that. All I'm saying is that I'm beginning to think it may work.'

Her heart felt light and as his lips touched hers she almost burst with happiness.

He moved back slightly to look down at her. 'You're so very beautiful.' His voice was thick and croaky. 'You must have this effect on every man you meet. Do you realise how dangerous you are and how easily a man can be drawn to you.'

She watched him, biting back tears. 'Is that so bad when it's you?'

His expression hardened. 'Yes.'

'But why, when we feel the way we do about each other?'

He shook his head. 'I don't want to hurt you, but it's only fair that I'm honest. I've lost my love. She drowned at sea with our child. I won't ever desert their memory. It was my fault. The least I can do is remain true to them.'

'Why was it your fault?' She had to know.

He stared at her, his eyes hardening. 'She died because of my stupidity. I might just as well have killed her. You can't understand. I don't even want you to. It's between me and Helen. I loved her, I still love her and if it wasn't for me she wouldn't be dead.' He was fighting with his emotions, his features twisted against the pain.

She watched as he stood up and

looked over the loch. After a few seconds he turned, came to her and enfolded her in his arms. 'The last thing I want is to hurt you. That was the main reason I wanted you to go back home. I have nothing to offer you, Vanessa. Friendship isn't enough, I know.'

He took her hand and they walked slowly round the loch, both silent in thought. Then he stopped and picking up a handful of pebbles began skimming them across the quiet water. Clouds were forming which finally obliterated the sun altogether and a dark foreboding clutched at Vanessa.

There was nothing she could think of to say. To move out of his life once and for all was the only answer and yet the pain was too great to contemplate and she wanted only to hold on to this moment when he was here with her.

His eyes still on the black water, he began to talk, more as if he was thinking aloud rather than to her. 'I used to come here when I was a child to think out my problems.' Then suddenly he turned to her, his expression changed.

'Look, if you want to go ahead with your plan on the island then I'll not put any obstacles in your way. I just simply don't know how you're going to do it. But if money is the problem then I can help there.'

'No,' she said quickly. 'Money is not a problem.' She began to relate everything that had happened the previous day. Despondency was partly relieved by the fact that, despite everything else, he was making it possible for her to stay close to him. Yet caution stopped her from depending too much on his co-operation.

He listened silently, his brows knitting and his smile fading. 'I see,' was all he said.

'I have the people and the money,' she began.

'So all you need is the place,' he finished for her and his look was challenging.

She met it head on. 'No, I don't need

a place. I can hire a hall for rehearsals and then take bookings through an agency. I should think there would be plenty of demand throughout the many islands up here.'

'You don't need to hire a hall,' he said tightly. 'I've already said you can use the ceilidh hall on the island.'

'No, you haven't said that,' she retorted.

He was becoming angry. 'Vanessa, I told you I won't stand in the way of your venture.'

'That's not the same thing.'

She was standing her ground firmly and he moved towards her and took her arm moving her towards him.

'Vanessa, why do you always provoke me? I'm offering you what you said you wanted. You can use the hall, perform on the island.'

She pulled free of his grasp. 'For how long, though? Until you decide to throw us all out again.' Her anger was rising. 'I can't trust you, Robert, and I'm no longer prepared to play into your hands. I've made my plans and I'm sticking to them. Once we have the show on the road then we'll visit your island if invited to do so but I won't put the whole project into jeopardy relying on your co-operation.'

His eyes blazed and he took hold of her again pulling her to him, their faces so close she could feel his hot breath and see the beads of perspiration on his forehead and cheeks.

Then his lips covered hers and he kissed her with a passion and then, moving her away from him yet still holding her firmly, he spoke with controlled intensity. 'Vanessa, have I ever deceived you? Do you honestly think I would trick you like that?'

She lowered her eyes from his tortured gaze.

He dropped his hold on her and all she could murmur was, 'I'm sorry.'

His whole posture registered despair and Vanessa felt regret that she had allowed her own vulnerability to manifest itself in such a vicious attack.

Above everything Robert had been honest with her, straight and honest. She stood awkwardly looking at him.

After a long silence he put his arm round her shoulders and began to guide her back to the castle.

Her brief farewell to Mary was painful.

'Take care of yourself until we meet again, dear,' Mary said. She was spared a final farewell with Robert as he was called into the estate office to take a telephone call.

Driving back to Mallaig behind Thomas, Vanessa stared out at the now black mountainous landscape as thunderclouds gathered and the first rain dropped heavily on the windscreen.

Robert's Emotions Remain Raw

Robert was at her hotel before she had finished breakfast next morning. He was bright and cheerful and she had difficulty in reconciling his present mood with their departure yesterday.

Taking her hand and guiding her back to her room he closed the door firmly.

'Angus will have the motor launch tied up this afternoon. He'll wait until you are ready to go — whenever that may be. Maude has been instructed to get Fisherman's Cottage ready for you, and Janice will put up all the rest of the actors at the hotel.'

He squeezed her arms when she didn't answer and the plea in his eyes caused her legs to weaken.

'Vanessa, I want you to go back to

the island and I know the island wants you.'

She did not doubt the second part of this statement and she wanted to believe the first.

'But Fisherman's Cottage is your home. I can't stay there.'

His control was slipping again and she could sense impatience and yet she couldn't risk placing herself under his power. She didn't even need the island.

After all the hard work, the setbacks and the doubts, she finally did have a good group of actors and the promise of sufficient funds to hire a hall and build a really successful touring theatre. She could direct it and produce the sort of plays which were important to her and she knew in her heart it was what she had always wanted.

He was still watching her face for a reply.

'I won't go back to the island until my group is ready to perform,' she said, summoning every shred of self-restraint she could muster.

His face was immobile. 'Fine, I'll tell Hettie.'

'Tell her what? What do you mean?'

He knew he'd won and a smile played behind his eyes.

'I'll tell her you don't want to go back to the island after all, that you've found something to suit you better. She'll be disappointed and I know the children were looking forward to the workshops you promised them, but I daresay they'll get over it.' With these parting comments he walked to the door and turned, the smile hardly contained now.

'That's emotional blackmail,' she seethed at him. 'You really know how to get to me, don't you?'

The smile came then as he turned the doorknob, still holding her gaze. 'It worked though, didn't it?' He went out and she heard him taking the stairs two at a time.

But they hadn't finished and she wasn't prepared to capitulate completely, so rushing after him, was out in the car park before he had time to rev up the engine.

She leaned through his open window. 'I shan't be ready this afternoon. Strange though you may find it I do have arrangements to make. And I don't want to stay in your cottage.'

'Why? What's wrong with it? Is it too primitive for you?'

'Of course not.'

'Then stay there.'

She wanted to scream at him but she was also tired of the arguments and just wanted to bring proceedings to an end. With both hands planted firmly on his opened windows she looked him in the eye.

'Robert, I'm not playing games this time. I have other people to consider.'

He returned her look, his eyes more serious now. 'I won't put any obstacles in your way, Vanessa. Do what you have to do and then if you decide you do want to go back to the island let me know and I'll send Angus for you.'

He scribbled a telephone number on

a scrap of paper and gave it to her and as she watched him drive away she cursed herself for again falling under his power.

★　★　★

So it was with mixed feelings that three weeks later Vanessa viewed the swirling mists over the mountains as the small boat pitched and tossed its way towards the island under Angus's expert handling.

After three weeks of hard work her plans were set. Shirley's father had been more generous than Vanessa could ever have hoped.

She had insisted on drawing up a proper contract whereby he would receive a fair percentage of the profits once they began to make any. He had shaken his head, 'Nay, lass, I've more than enough to keep body and soul together. Now if tha' can make a success o' it and keep my Shirl, here, happy, then tha's welcome to lot.' But eventually he had respected her wishes and made a business-like agreement.

During the three weeks she had continued to stay at the hotel in Mallaig and had heard nothing more from Robert. True to his word he had not made problems for her. In fact she had received every co-operation through his staff on the estate. But every time she used the telephone number he had given her she had to deal with others and never got to speak to Robert, himself.

Now she was nearing the island to settle into Fisherman's Cottage and make ready for the arrival, within the next few days, of the rest of the group.

The sky was an angry grey and a cold mist swirled round the peaks, and so many memories flooded back, of the storm at sea when Robert had edged her in to land and she had not understood his fears for her. And yet he didn't care for her enough to put his past behind him and love her.

The boat tossed and heaved and Vanessa was soaked from the spray coming over the side.

'Will you not shelter below?' Angus asked with concern.

'No, I prefer to be up here in the open,' she said.

'Well, you must like this island fine to want to come back so badly,' he said.

'Have you seen Robert lately?' she asked.

'No, he doesn't come over now he has the estate to manage. The man's got a lot on his plate these days,' he said, dispelling the slight hope she had that Robert may be waiting at the cottage for her.

'And what about the others?' she enquired. 'Is Hettie back at school yet?'

'She will be after the holiday. The strange one they sent over did noot but moan. At the end of term she was away back home.'

They neared the jetty and Vanessa could see several people waiting to welcome her back. Steven took her bag and put it in the back of his Land Rover. 'Janice insists you come up to the hotel for a meal before you settle in,' he told her and they drove off up on to the road.

Over homemade steak and kidney pudding, Janice filled her in on all the news. The hotel was ready for her friends now and Robert had actually subsidised some of the refurbishment. Most of the cottages were occupied by summer visitors. The ceilidh hall had been redecorated — much to the amazement of the islanders, and a small generator installed for extra stage lighting.

'Robert really is pulling out all the stops for you,' Janice said and Vanessa felt a warm glow inside her.

'Everyone is so excited about your plans and the children want to see you as soon as possible. You've no idea what a difference it will make to the life here. I just don't know why Robert was so against it in the first place,' Janice said. 'Once the hotel gets booked up and your theatre starts we'll have this place buzzing.'

'I'm not too sure that Robert would allow that,' she laughed. 'You know, I can't remember when I last enjoyed a meal so much. It's as if months of stress are falling away.'

Janice smiled. 'You really do look so much better. You're like a young, carefree girl again.'

There had been evenings like this with Greg and Felicity and Denise in the old Cheltern Theatre. A shadow crossed her face and Janice noticed.

'Your friends will all be here soon.'

'Yes, except Greg.' She couldn't help wishing he was coming too.

'Come on, my love, it's time I drove you home. It's nearly midnight.' Steven said.

'If there's anything you want, now, just let us know,' Janice said giving her a hug.

Alone in Fisherman's Cottage memories came flooding back and Vanessa wondered why Robert had let her use his own cottage.

'All the others are occupied,' Janice

had told her when she had voiced concern. 'It saves him trying to rearrange bookings.'

Wandering into the bedroom, she opened the wardrobe doors and saw his shirts and jumpers, a couple of pairs of old jeans and his one smart suit. There were photos of Helen and Joe, ornaments, the bed he slept on, now freshly made up for her. Maude had cleaned through it thoroughly ready for her arrival but she hadn't been able to remove the essence of the man. It touched Vanessa in every room and she longed for him to be there with her.

She picked up the photograph of Helen and studied it, a soft, feminine face full of indulgent understanding. Helen would have pampered him, indulged his every whim and never argued. Vanessa knew she could never fulfil a role like that.

She slowly unzipped her bag and stowed her few clothes away in what available space she could find. With the addition of only a few warm jumpers and a pair of stout shoes she had only the clothes she had arrived with when she had thought she was coming for three weeks holiday. And, of course, the red dress Robert had bought for her.

Hanging it carefully in the wardrobe beside his light suit she wondered what had possessed him to indulge her with this flimsy dress. Then she closed the wardrobe door against the pain.

After making coffee in his kitchen she sat at the wooden table and wondered why she felt so depressed. Everything was going well. The others would be arriving over the next couple of days and there was work to be done. Her plans were about to come to fruition. But when she eventually slid between the clean white sheets in Robert's big double bed the tears began to roll.

Felicity, Denise and Ken arrived next morning and after settling in at the hotel they all gathered in the newly decorated ceilidh hall and began to plan their first rehearsal of *Moonshine*.

'I like it,' Ken told her. 'Lots of

action and good lines.'

'Too many,' Felicity grumbled, but Vanessa knew she would already be word perfect.

In loose trousers, tee shirt and canvas pumps Vanessa worked like a Trojan. Alan and Shirley arrived two days later and slid into the already established routine like true professionals.

'Heavens, how are we ever going to turn this into a theatre?' Shirley asked, viewing the bare hall.

'Like the true troupers we are,' Felicity laughed.

'We said we wanted a new challenge, didn't we?' Ken observed. 'Denise is very resourceful, you know.'

Denise gave him a playful shove. 'Have to be, working with you lot. I like the new spotlights, they'll certainly make a difference.'

The whole group gelled as Vanessa knew they would. Over the next week the play began to come to life and they all enjoyed the rehearsals immensely. Vanessa was too worn out when she returned at night to Fisherman's Cottage to feel lonely and was grateful for the quiet peace of it.

Between rehearsals she had been to the school and set up holiday work-shops for the children.

'Come and have a cup of tea with me,' Hettie said one day when they had finished. Vanessa was taking her second piece of fruit loaf, a special Scottish recipe at which Hettie excelled, when the conversation came round to Robert again.

'I don't suppose we'll see much of him here now,' Hettie said resignedly.

Vanessa felt a pang of anxiety. 'He's sure to come back, once he's got things sorted out after his father's death. He's too fond of the island to desert it for long.'

The old lady was pensive. 'Yes, you're probably right. He's too sensitive for his own good, that boy. When he was a wee lad and came over on holidays he was always wandering over the heath and watching the wildlife. I sometimes wonder whether he'll ever get over his wife's death. It was a tragic affair.'

Vanessa held her breath and determined that now was the time if she was ever to get to the truth of what happened.

'Why does he feel so guilty about it?' she asked.

Hettie looked surprised. 'He told you that, did he? Or have you been listening to the tittle tattle of the locals.'

Vanessa wondered if she had betrayed a confidence but she trusted Hettie and she needed someone to talk to about Robert.

Hettie shook her head. 'I suppose I might as well tell you as you're not the type to gossip. And besides, you may be able to help him. You've obviously got closer to him than most, and the lad does need help if he's ever to have a life again.'

Vanessa felt her heart pounding as Hettie continued. 'He feels it was his fault and he'll never forgive himself or give himself a moment's peace. You see, he had removed the radio from the boat. It needed repairing and he'd taken it out but hadn't warned Helen. It was simply an oversight but he thinks that if he had not done it they could have been saved. He can't rid his mind of the picture of them both trapped in a sinking boat with no radio to rely on to call up assistance. It will plague his mind for the rest of his life.'

Lines of distress distorted Hettie's kind face as she spoke.

Vanessa felt her throat tighten and her hands were shaking. In fact she was shivering uncontrollably at the thought of the agony Robert must have lived through and still suffered.

'But he didn't know they were going out that morning. He told me the weather was dreadful and not fit for anyone to go to sea,' she whispered.

Hettie looked at her, her brows knitted. 'I know that, we all know that. Helen was foolish to have taken the child out that morning. Nobody knows why she did it, why she took the risk, especially without telling Robert or anyone else she was going. It was not Robert's fault and nobody blamed him, except himself.'

Hettie was becoming so upset by the conversation that Vanessa felt bound to end it and resume a more cheerful topic for fear of bringing on another heart attack, but there were still unanswered questions that bothered her. Why was Helen so careless for herself and her son that fateful morning?

It played on her mind so much that when Maude came to give the cottage its usual Thursday morning clean, Vanessa, though still fearful of the woman, did try once more to bring her into a civil conversation.

'You really don't need to clean for me,' she ventured. 'I have plenty of time between rehearsals and it's a very small cottage. I'm sure you have plenty to do at the guest house now that the season is in full swing.'

'I've always gone through it once a week and I'll continue to do so,' she snapped.

Trying to bring out some warmth in her nature, Vanessa looked towards a photograph of Helen on the wall.

'She was very beautiful, your daughter, and so like Morag.'

'Yes,' was the curt reply and Maude flicked her duster furiously.

Vanessa regretted her tactlessness in approaching what must be such a painful subject.

But Maude seemed eager now to continue and, as she beat the cushions into submission, started a tirade. 'It was no accident. My Helen knew boats too well. Maybe you've been told differently. But I know it was not an accident.'

Vanessa watched the angry woman and wished she had left well alone. She didn't want to hear any more but Maude was looking straight at her. 'You want to keep clear of that family. They're evil.'

Vanessa was shocked and Maude must have realised she had said too much so quickly modified her statement. 'Not Robert. I don't mean Robert. He's a good man. Looked after Morag and me since the tragedy and he's promised that he always will. My Morag's very fond of Robert.' There was a depth of meaning in this last sentence and Vanessa took it as a warning.

Maude looked at her sharply and then continued to clatter round the kitchen banging cupboard doors with unnecessary vigour.

Rather than clarify things, the conversation only mystified Vanessa more than ever. Whilst most of her time and effort over the next few days was devoted to getting their first play knocked into shape, whenever her mind was free to wonder, it puzzled over what had really happened to Helen.

The more she thought about it the more she realised just how much she cared about Robert, how much she really loved him. Whatever had happened in the past made no difference to her feelings for him and more than anything she wished she could share all his confused and guilty feelings.

He was so much on her mind that when he suddenly appeared in her life again it was as if she had been expecting him.

After a long day of rehearsals she had popped into the store to buy some groceries and found the shop closed and Fiona nursing a bad migraine and fretting over where Jamie had got to on his bike.

'Angus should have been back long since and then I could have asked him to watch the wee laddie while I lay down for a while. It's the only cure when I'm taken like this. And Jamie is such a chatterbox.'

Vanessa shook her head and smiled at the inevitable. Tired though she was she would have to help out. 'I'll find him and take him down to the beach for an hour.'

Fiona put up a restraining hand and then winced in pain. 'I didn't mean that. No, I'll manage just fine. Now, you go on home and rest yourself. You look fair done in.'

Vanessa stopped her. 'Fiona, I need the fresh air to clear my own head after a day shut up in that hall.'

She found Jamie rounding the corner on his way home and suggested they go down to the beach. So it was while she was attempting to fly a kite on an open stretch of sand that Robert appeared.

'The tail's not heavy enough,' the deep voice said over her shoulder and she jumped with shock. 'Needs a bit of paper or something,' he continued. 'Here, this bit of seaweed may work.'

Dressed in jeans and T-shirt, his hair blowing in the wind, he was the carefree man she had first known when she arrived on the island. Soon the kite was well and truly launched and Jamie happily tugging at the string.

'Quite the expert,' she commented, her heart bursting with happiness at seeing him again.

They walked over to an outcrop of rocks and sat together watching the waves pounding up the beach.

'I've missed you,' he said taking her hand.

She looked up into his sensitive face and dark eyes and smiled. All she ever wanted was this. If only time could stand still so that she could be with Robert sharing this closeness always.

'How's the play going?' he asked.

'Very well. We're hoping to put on the first performance in a fortnight. I've already had enquiries from three other islands asking for us to stage a production for them. I really think it's going to be successful.'

'I'm very pleased,' he said and she knew he meant it.

'Why were you so against it to start with?' she asked.

He looked at her somewhat surprised. 'I just didn't think it would be right for the island. I told you. I didn't take much to your friends and I thought you'd put on some trashy show and turn the place into a holiday camp. But then I saw how serious you were and I knew I could trust you.' He paused. 'And I didn't want you to go away.'

She knew then that this last reason was his main reason for allowing her to do what, in his heart, he did not approve of, and it made her more determined than ever not to let him down, to produce the sort of plays he would enjoy and approve of. But for now, just knowing he wanted her here was enough and she ached for his kiss, the feel of his arms around her and the closeness of his body against hers.

The kite got tangled on the rocks and Robert leapt up to free it. Vanessa watched his lithe body and the enjoyment he derived from playing with Jamie, and her thoughts went back to the son he once had.

Throughout the next hour they stayed on the beach with Jamie, their passion growing with every touch and look.

Eventually they clambered up the rocks to the road where Robert had parked the truck and drove to the store to deposit Jamie. Angus was home and Robert had a long conversation with him while Vanessa sat in the truck becoming increasingly impatient and tense.

She now had time to wonder why Robert had come back to the island, and more to the point, where he intended to stay.

The drive back to the cottage was full of tension, Vanessa not daring to ask what his plans were for fear of disappointment and Robert not appearing to want to divulge them.

'You look tired,' he said once they had unlocked themselves from the first embrace inside the cottage. 'Why don't you have a nice long soak in the bath while I cook us a meal; that's of course if you have anything to cook and don't mind me taking charge of your kitchen.'

Vanessa was glad she'd bought the chicken from Fiona and gratefully accepted his offer.

Soaking in hot soapy bubbles, she listened to Robert in the kitchen humming softly and felt utter contentment.

It was while she was drying her hair in the bedroom that he knocked on the door. 'Can I come in?' he asked.

'You can come in,' she answered.

He came up behind her and looked at her in the mirror as she brushed her hair into soft curls. Then he turned her towards him and took her in his arms. She was still holding the hairdryer so he gently removed it from her hand and threw it carelessly on to the bed without taking his eyes from hers.

The splintering of glass brought them both back to their senses and she looked down at the broken photograph frame. The dryer had caught it and toppled it off the small shelf, missing the rug and crashing on to the stone floor. Robert stared at it for a moment, and then carefully bent and extracted the photograph of Helen and Joe.

In stone-like silence he looked at it and then without a word or a look at Vanessa he left the room, the photograph held closely to his chest.

Vanessa sat rigid for a long time, pain replacing the pleasure, and then eventually she got heavily off the bed and walked through to the living room.

He was sitting beside the embers of a dying fire staring at the photograph, his face immobile. She knelt beside him and touched his arm but he withdrew it sharply.

'I want to understand,' she said quietly.

He looked at her strangely as if he was confused as to why she was there.

'Understand?' he said. 'Nobody can do that. It's between Helen and me. It doesn't matter to anyone else.'

Tears were threatening and her voice would hardly come. 'But Helen isn't here now and I am. Can't you share it with me?'

Again he looked at the photograph and then back at her as if lost in a world of his own.

'Helen would have liked you. You're everything she wasn't. She was shy and quiet, not clever but very pretty and very loving. She admired people like you, go ahead people like Fiona and Hettie. But she never envied them and was always herself.'

'She wouldn't have wanted you to be miserable,' Vanessa said. 'She wouldn't have wanted you to cut yourself off from life and never to love again.' She stopped, feeling she'd said too much.

He shook his head. 'It's not that, Vanessa. I just wouldn't want to make anyone else as unhappy as I made her.'

Vanessa was shocked and tried to stop him but he was determined to carry on. 'You want to know why, well I'll tell you. My parents wouldn't accept Helen, at least my father wouldn't. Mother didn't have much say in the matter. She tried to bring him round but had no success. He wouldn't visit, took no interest in my affairs, until he suddenly realised he was a sick man and had no heir. My sisters didn't count and I was in his bad books.

'So he decided that he would take Joe and educate him to be a suitable heir to the Kilmorgan estate. This meant school in Aberdeen and holidays at Kilmorgan Castle. Helen was devastated at the idea.' He stopped.

'But you wouldn't have let it happen, surely?' Vanessa was stunned.

'No, I don't think I would. But I listened. I considered it. There was nothing on the island for Joe as he grew older. He was a bright, intelligent boy who needed companions of his own age and a proper education. I was tempted.'

His voice was tight, his agitation growing. He stood up and paced the room. 'I didn't listen to Helen. I put forward all my arguments until she felt betrayed. She wasn't very good at arguing. I do this, you see, Vanessa. I can't see other people's point of view. I could never get on with my family, and then I didn't understand Helen. I'm just no good with people and I won't ever get involved again. I couldn't ever hurt anyone like that again.'

'What happened?' Her heart was thumping.

He looked at her, hurt and anger mixed in his eyes. 'Don't you ever give up? I've never talked like this to anyone before.'

'It will help,' she said, unconvinced that she was doing anything now other than persecuting herself as well as him, but somehow feeling that he must talk and she must listen.

He was looking at her straight now, his eyes piercing and she felt frightened. His voice was menacingly controlled. 'I wouldn't listen to her pleas. The night before she took Joe out in the boat she was beside herself with worry and fear, pleading with me to promise I wouldn't allow Joe to be taken away. I told her to calm herself, to be more reasonable, that we would talk it through when she had quietened down, and I went out.

'Hours later when I came back home she was calm, happy almost. I didn't bring the subject up again and neither did she. And then early in the morning when I woke she was sleeping peacefully. She hadn't planned the trip, the weather was totally unsuitable, and it was a school day. So I went off to help Angus with the sheep. Do I need to say more?' His blunt, matter of fact tone was unnerving.

'I don't believe she took her own life, or endangered Joe,' Vanessa whispered.

His eyes blazed anger. 'No, you wouldn't. Neither does anyone else. They all try to convince me it was an accident. But they don't know what went on. They don't know how I treated her. They don't know what a monster my family has bred.'

He slammed around the room banging his fists on the table and mantelpiece until she thought he would wreck the place. Then drawing himself together he gave her one final withering look and walked out of the door and into the night.

Vanessa gazed after him, unable to think or move, until finally she sank into a chair by the fire. She picked up the photograph he had dropped beside him and looked at the large pool like eyes and an involuntary shiver of apprehension came over her. There was something in that face she had not seen before.

Vanessa's Acting Dream Is Realised

Vanessa found it almost impossible to concentrate the next day. But their first performance was to take place on Saturday in the ceilidh hall and her professionalism would not allow her to let down her group of actors who had put so much effort into ensuring it would be a success.

She had no idea where Robert had gone to after leaving Fisherman's Cottage late last night and it played on her mind all day.

'This chair just won't do,' Felicity moaned. 'How can I keep sitting and getting up elegantly when there are no springs and I sink down to the floor.'

'Easy chairs aren't easy to come by on an island like this,' Denise admonished. 'You'll just have to practice. The exercise will do you good.'

Felicity's eyes blazed fury. Vanessa could feel the sparks beginning to fly and knew she had to cool the situation but wished she didn't have to cope with these tedious arguments. 'I'll get Angus to bring one round from the cottage,' she said.

By the time they had finished at three o'clock in the afternoon, Vanessa's head ached with weariness due to lack of sleep. The hall had become stuffy and when she walked outside the fresh air was wonderful. The July sun was hot with a gently cooling breeze from the sea so she decided to walk back via the harbour rather than take the more direct route home, not anxious to be locked away in the cottage with memories of last night.

Wild flowers grew in profusion and the tiny lambs had filled out into almost the size of their mothers and no longer clung so timidly. She slipped off her shoes and paddled in the clear stream. But her heart ached.

The harbour was peaceful with one or two yachts moored, the sea reflecting metallically in the high sun. She saw his fishing boat lying at anchor not far from the quay and knew instinctively that Robert was on board. That was where he had spent the night. So he hadn't returned to Mallaig as she had expected.

She was about to turn up the path back to the cottage and privacy when Morag noticed her from the teashop and rushed up to her, her face angry. 'Have you two been arguing?' she said, her eyes dark and direct.

Vanessa was taken aback, not certain what Morag meant or sure that she wanted her involved. But Morag was determined. 'I saw him rush off last night. I was baking here late on and I called to him but he wouldn't answer. He was just hell bent on reaching his boat.' She stopped, searching Vanessa's face for a reaction. 'He's a fool to himself, that man. Vanessa, I really thought that you and him — ' She tailed off.

Vanessa was grateful for the direct approach and sensed her sincerity. 'I thought so, too.'

That was all Morag needed. 'You must not let him go, Vanessa. He thinks he owes so much to us all. To myself and Mother and everyone in the community.

'Although he's never spoken openly about it I know he blames himself for what happened to Helen. He thinks she killed herself because of some argument they had. It's all stupid. Helen was always unbalanced. She'd tried to commit suicide several times but Mother caught her in time and this was long before she knew Robert.'

Vanessa remembered the photograph of Helen and knew now what had disturbed her about the face. It was the eyes. They were Morag's eyes but instead of being large and beautiful, in Helen they were strangely staring.

'We've all tried to talk to him,' Morag continued. 'Now you are his last chance. He's crazy about you, everyone can see that. He's never taken so much interest in anyone since Helen died. You've just got to make him see sense.'

'But how?' Vanessa asked helplessly. 'I didn't know about any of this until last night, and I did try to talk to him, but I felt like an intruder. I don't really think he does want anyone else in his life.'

'Of course he does,' Morag snapped. 'He probably needs time, but please, Vanessa, don't give up on him. We're all terribly fond of Robert.'

She smiled. 'Even Mother is really, though she was hoping he would settle for me after Helen, especially as we're so alike, but don't let her put you off. I'm not after him, but I would like to see him happy again.'

Vanessa was finding it difficult to cope with this conversation. So many strange feelings were creeping around inside her. She glanced again at the boat. And then she stared helplessly as it increased its distance between them. The two women just watched it skim the water and quickly become a speck in the distance.

'Blast the man,' Morag cursed and Vanessa tried desperately to control the panic she felt inside, so quickly turned and ran up the hill towards Fisherman's Cottage.

Robert had seen the two women talking and knew he had to get away. Now on the open sea he could breathe again. But there wasn't a sense of peace he usually found. His mind was in turmoil. He wanted her, needed her. How could he spend the rest of his life knowing she was out there somewhere, living an independent life away from him, and he was here living with his memories and his guilt? Yet he couldn't break free. Guilt would not let him. He was responsible for Helen's death and he had to live with it.

Back in the cottage Vanessa began to tidy the kitchen and find something to eat in sheer determination to keep going.

How could she pursue a man who lived in a remote castle in the Scottish Highlands? How was she supposed to even communicate with him?

Despite what Morag had told her she was not convinced she could succeed in changing his mind anyway and her confidence was dwindling all the time until she was certain that nobody could replace Helen.

Try as she would to put everything out of her mind and concentrate on preparing a meal and eating it, hunger was far from her and she stared at the food on her plate. She must get on with her life and just let Robert make up his own mind. If she forced him into a decision, he might live to resent it and resent her, and anyway she knew he was too strong-minded ever to do anything he didn't want to do.

After Saturday's show there would be arrangements to make to travel to the other islands that had shown an interest. She would have her work cut out putting the whole venue on a proper business footing so that the money they had been lent by Shirley's father could be paid back.

It would have been an exciting time. If only she could rid her mind and her heart of all the longing and ache which prevented her from properly enjoying her own success.

The next couple of days passed in a flurry of rehearsals and organisation in the hall, but still in the odd quiet moments her mind would drift back to their last evening together.

Denise took her to one side. 'Vanessa, what's worrying you. The play's going fine, you know.'

'It's not that,' Vanessa confided.

'What then?' Denise encouraged gently.

'It's Robert,' she confessed.

Denise nodded slowly. 'I knew there was something. Who is that young man? He brought you to The Hole when we were staying there, didn't he? Have you two got something going?'

'No, I thought we did, but he's not interested. Denise, don't say anything to the others, will you? I can't stand teasing just now.'

'Don't worry, love, I won't say a word.' And she knew Denise wouldn't.

But how could she go through all the events of the next months not knowing what Robert was feeling, how he was suffering, whether he needed her? And yet he knew where she was. All he had to do was come to her. She'd given him every indication that he would be more than welcome. But he hadn't come. That must mean that he really didn't want her in his life.

Yet Morag had been so sure that he did. And she had felt so, too. But how could she know for sure? Round and round her thoughts went until at last she felt some course of action was necessary, if only to preserve her own sanity.

Denise was constantly watching her and always ready to listen without giving unwanted advice.

'I'm going to send him an invitation to the play,' Vanessa told her. 'What do you think? It seems a perfectly normal and polite thing to do, to invite the laird of the island to our first performance.'

Denise smiled warmly. 'I think it's a grand idea.'

'It will give him the opportunity to come and see me again or politely refuse,' Vanessa said.

By Saturday nerves were taut. 'No, Angus, we can't have chairs there; that is where the trestle tables go for the food,' Maude chided.

Angus continued to put out another row in the ceilidh hall. 'We have a hundred and fifty to seat, woman. Where else will I put them?'

'Don't you take that tone with me. When Morag brings the food this afternoon she'll be bothering me about where to put it.'

'We don't need food for this do. It's a proper play, not one of our home spun efforts. Now leave me be while I find some more seats.'

'Angus, we don't have any more seats,' Maude snapped. 'How can we have that many coming? There is not that many on the island.'

'But there are. The hotel is full and all the cottages are occupied. Is your guest house not full?'

'Of course, my place is always full, but we still cannot have that many.'

'I'm telling you, woman, that that is how many are expected.'

'So are we to magic some out of thin air? I doubt even our wonderful actors can do that,' she said sarcastically.

'Well, that's where you're wrong now, because our wonderful actors have done just that. We are to have folk come from all the islands. So now perhaps you'll get away with you and leave a man in peace to do his job.'

His self-satisfied smirk brought a look of disdain from Maude. She huffed and went off to find Morag.

'What is that man talking about, telling me we are to expect a hundred and fifty? We'll be lucky to fill the seats he has out already,' she told Morag.

'No, Mother, it is so. They're coming from everywhere to see our play. Angus is to fetch a party this afternoon and some are arriving from the mainland on the afternoon ferry. Janice has had to make up extra beds in some of the old bedrooms. It's to be a big event, there's a lot of interest in this new company. Robert is even allowing some to camp on the Dunnin field.'

'And where is the food to go?'

'We are only to have tea and biscuits this time. There are too many to cater for.'

'Well, it's come to something when we cannot offer proper hospitality to our guests.'

Maude stared in disbelief at her daughter then shuffled off tutting.

For Vanessa there was the extra anxiety of whether Robert would appear and how she would feel at seeing him again. Would he behave formally or give her that special look, which would let her know he still cared and that he had come because he had wanted to, not because he felt he should put in an appearance?

When the doors opened at seven

o'clock there was a queue outside and by seven fifteen every seat was taken.

'Vanessa. They're pouring in,' Felicity squeaked. 'Angus, we must have some more seats.'

'Don't fret, lass. We've some benches at the back and the wee ones can sit on the floor in front.'

Eventually everyone was in the hall and seated. As silence fell and the lights dimmed an atmosphere of anticipation fell on the hall. Newly installed spotlights lit the stage and the actors came on to a hushed audience.

A seat in the front row was reserved for Robert but by the interval it was still empty.

'I see His Royal Highness hasn't turned up,' Felicity said, and there were other good-natured comments about the empty seat, but most of the conversation was enthusiastic approval of the play and the calibre of the acting.

Despite her disappointment Vanessa found a warm glow of pride growing within her.

'You've a grand company of actors there,' the doctor told her during the interval.

'Aye, it's a fine play you've put together,' Angus said.

'Could we not be in it next time?' Jamie asked Vanessa.

Fiona smiled indulgently. 'You're a fine little actor, and no mistake. You know how to twist me round your little finger, anyhow.'

Vanessa gave him a hug. 'Next time you'll be up on that stage, I promise.'

It was a resounding success. Bookings were coming in for future venues and the problem was going to be fitting them all in. Her intuition had proved correct, the islands did want entertainment and her new company had hit on the right formula. Their future success was guaranteed.

Full of pride and totally exhausted, she refused Angus's offer of a lift home in the Land Rover in order to walk back to the cottage in the cool, clear air.

The moon was high and gave the

land a haunting silver hue. The rough track led through the copse where she had first seen Robert chopping logs. A heaviness settled on her as she thought of how much Robert was a part of this island, how he had lived and loved on it and how great tragedy had struck and transformed his life, and how it still occupied a special corner of his heart.

How she wished she could find a spot in his heart and share his love of this place. Would she ever forget, or even resign herself to the fact that it was all over?

She turned up and on to the cliff path and paused to watch the waves breaking on the rocks, white foam spraying silver in the moonlight. It was haunting, it was magic. Her heart was as much on this island as Robert's.

With just the roar of the waves and the cry of night birds on the cliffs, she slowly and reluctantly made her way nearer to the cottage.

As soon as it came into sight she knew with uncanny certainty that it was not empty. There were no visible signs; no light or parked vehicle. The doors were closed and the curtains open, just as she had left them. And yet she knew.

Laying Ghosts Of The Past To Rest

Her heart began to pound and her hands felt clammy as she lightened her step and quietly opened the gate. Lifting the latch of the unlocked door, she let herself into the living-room and saw his dark form silhouetted against the moonlit window.

He turned and spoke as she came in, his voice deep and soft. 'I'm sorry, Vanessa, I didn't mean to alarm you. I hope you don't mind me letting myself in.'

'It is your cottage,' she said, trying to make her voice sound normal. She lit the gas lamp over the fireplace and in the soft glow his eyes sought and held hers.

'You didn't come to the concert.' She tried desperately to make it sound matter of fact, still not certain why he was here.

'No, I didn't want us to meet in public, not after the way I left you. What I have to say to you must be said privately, that's why I came here and waited for you.'

Her heart was pounding so loudly she was sure he must be able to hear it.

'I've come back to say goodbye,' he said.

She stopped breathing. No, he couldn't, not after the way he had looked at her, building up her hope. She couldn't bear it. Tears were coming, they threatened to flood out and she wanted to rage and scream and beat him into sense, but all she did was stare at his face dry eyed.

He pulled her down beside him on the sofa and continued in his soft lilting voice. 'I've done a lot of thinking since I left you. My thoughts have been so confused recently.'

She tried to edge away from him but he held her firmly. 'Robert, don't spin it out. Just say goodbye and go, please.'

'Vanessa, I need to explain. Please listen. Until you came along it was straightforward. I had resigned myself to the loss of my wife and son, resigned myself to living with the guilt and to devoting the rest of my life to helping Helen's family and the whole island.'

'Robert, I don't want to take you away from that. I do understand.'

'No, you don't. This somehow gave life a purpose and made it easier to cope. You disturbed all that. You made me feel alive again and see that there was more. I tried to see you as a friend in order to make our relationship innocent, no threat to my conscience. When that didn't work I tried to avoid you, get you out of my life altogether.'

'I'm leaving anyway,' she put in quickly. 'I'm sorry, I didn't realise the way it was when I persisted in this venture. But we're all moving on now. Please, just let us leave and forget we were ever here.'

His brow knit and he studied her

slowly. 'I thought you might feel like that and I don't blame you. You're a great success and I should have had more faith, but I wasn't acting rationally at the time.'

All she wanted was to terminate this conversation, pack her bags and leave. The explanations were like a knife turning ever deeper into the wound.

'Vanessa, it really is important to me that I explain to you. Then you can walk away. I won't stop you.'

The words were pouring out now as she resigned herself to hear him out.

'There's a lot you don't know about Helen, how she was. She had her moods and she would withdraw at times but it was part of her nature. She was a lovely, gentle woman, easily hurt and Vanessa, I hurt her.'

He looked away and out through the window a the sea. 'I hurt her so much and was so insensitive as not to even realise what I was putting her through. But there's more, a lot more.' He looked directly at Vanessa. 'I don't know whether she took her own life or whether it was an accident.'

The words were forced out in an agony of torment and before she had time to argue with him he was continuing, talking fast.

'There was no radio on the boat when she set sail. She couldn't call up for help when things went wrong even if she'd wanted to. I don't know, Vanessa. I'll never know what was going on in her mind but I do know it was my fault. Either way it was my fault.

'She was beside herself at the thought of Joe being taken away from her; she probably thought in her own way she would take Joe with her where nobody could ever take him from her. And I drove her to that. But if she had wanted help she couldn't have called for it. I took the radio out. She had no radio on board.'

Vanessa wanted to stop him but her nerves were steadying and her mind edging quickly into gear, realising that this was her last chance. Not to capture

Robert for herself, her love for him went beyond the selfish pursuit of gain. She wanted desperately to free him from a life sentence of guilt if it was in her power, and talking it out was the only way.

She took his hand, firmly determined now that he would not pull away from her. 'Robert, stop torturing yourself. Helen knew boats. She'd been brought up on this island and had sailed all her life. She would have checked the safety equipment before she set off. People do drown at sea even when they do have radios. It does happen in severe weather. She may have made an error of judgement in going out when the weather was threatening, but lots of people do that as well.'

He wasn't listening to reason. 'I removed the radio, the most vital piece of safety equipment on any boat. I took it up to the house a week before to overhaul. It wasn't functioning properly. I should have returned it. At least I should have warned her that it was missing. I should have fixed it and returned it before she went out.'

'Did you know she wanted to go out?'

'No, not that day. The weather was terrible. There was no way she should have gone. I still can't understand why she did go except that I'd hurt her so much.'

'Robert, you're going round in circles,' she shouted at him. 'Helen was upset, she went out in the boat without going through the normal safety procedure and she took your son with her on a school day when the weather was totally unsuitable. The fact that you had a disagreement is nothing, how many marriages exist without them? You took the radio out of your boat to mend because it was broken, doesn't every boat owner do the same thing?'

She continued the tirade, not letting him interrupt and not sparing his feelings. She loved the man and she had to get through to him now whatever the consequences.

So she pressed on without taking a breath. 'She was unstable, Robert. Morag told me and you've got to believe it. You can't go blaming yourself forever. Helen had tried to take her own life before and fortunately her mother had been able to save her. But it was not your fault. You're wallowing in self-pity. You think you're so important that everyone falls apart if you upset them, that everything that goes wrong is because of something you've done. Don't you ever give anyone any credit for anything, not even for making their own mistakes?'

He was staring at her angrily but his eyes had lost their haunted look and she feared he was going to slap her face. For a long moment they faced each other, their eyes blazing fury and love, and suddenly he leant forward and pulled her roughly to him and buried his face in her hair.

They clung to each other and Vanessa wanted the world to stop, for in Robert's arms she felt complete. Every part of her life was unimportant and she could not visualise a future without his strength surrounding her.

Eventually he set her away from him but his eyes never left her face and with a lingering look he rose and walked from the cottage.

She stood in stunned disbelief and watched him pace down the path and away from her, his form silhouetted in the moonlight. As soon as he was on the track leading down the cliff his pace quickened and she felt utter despair knowing this was the end.

He would never come back to her now. She had lost him just when they had seemed to have found each other. He had held her in his arms as if he would never let her go and his eyes had spoken of love.

A lifetime now would separate them and Vanessa struggled to prevent the hysteria threatening to overpower her.

Suddenly the pain was unbearable, as Robert became a small shape in the distance and she knew even now she could not give up on him; she could not let him go.

All her strength gathered into pursuing this object and she rushed out of the cottage and with great speed and agility began to descend the path after him.

Her loose skirt and flat shoes facilitated quick movement but he was also accelerating and the distance between them was increasing.

If he moved out of sight she might lose him, and though she presumed he was heading for the quay nothing was ever certain with Robert. And anyway, it was imperative she reached him before he launched his boat and disappeared.

Putting every effort she could muster into speeding up, she just managed to keep him in sight. But he did not continue along the path to the quay, instead turning off and beginning to climb the alternate path leading inland.

Once on this route his pace slowed and Vanessa soon gained on him but something made her slow down too, and she followed at a discreet distance. They continued along the path, Vanessa feeling more and more uneasy as her suspicion strengthened, and when he turned off on to the small footpath she froze, knowing now for certain that her intuition had been correct.

Her desire for his look, his touch, his need, were like an invisible thread drawing her towards him.

When the tiny church came into view he stopped and she stopped and, still unaware that he was being followed, Robert was motionless for several minutes. Then he slowly continued up the path, through the gate and into the old churchyard.

In the silvery light she watched as he knelt down on the ground beside the gravestone and Vanessa sensed he was speaking softly, and her heart ached unbearably both for Robert and herself.

The moon was bright on the still water and, looking out to sea, Vanessa knew the pain in Robert's heart and his need to be constantly in touch with it. If only she could share it with him, so that however bad it was he would not suffer alone.

At least Robert could go to the church and be near to Helen. He had his memories and he'd had his love. What did she have? A successful career, and promising future, freedom?

How could she go on for a whole lifetime knowing that the only man she ever loved was married to a memory?

Married to a memory! She couldn't let the man she loved spend the rest of his life like that. She wouldn't.

Turning abruptly, she ran up the beach and scrambled up the rocks hell bent on gaining the path back to the church in the quickest possible time. Then she saw his figure approaching her. She stopped for a second and then with resolve walked slowly to meet him.

Their eyes met in the night brightness and held each other in silence.

Vanessa knew that this was to be the hardest task of her life and yet the way his eyes held her made success seem certain.

Before she spoke a word he took both her hands tightly.

'I knew I was right,' he whispered.

'About what?' she ventured.

'Vanessa, do you think you can cope with all this? With me?'

She hardly dared to breathe. What was he saying? She just couldn't afford to let her hopes run away with her again, so subdued her rising excitement and forced her voice to normality.

'Robert, what are you asking me?'

His eyes were the deepest brown she had ever seen and his face so intense.

'I'm asking you if you will marry me.'

All her joy exploded and she flung her arms round his neck and he lifted her in the air and then began to kiss her fervently and then with a deeper passion. She melted into him beneath the blue light of an early dawn. She had won his trust and nothing would ever part them again.

Eventually their faces parted and he

was smiling down at her, his face transformed, the dark curls damp on his forehead. 'I take it that means yes.'

Her mood was as light as his now. 'Just try to escape again and you'll soon find out.'

Again he pulled her to him and nestling against his strong body she felt she had belonged there always. Then she drew away, thoughtful for a moment, and looked at him.

What did you mean just then when you said you were right?' she asked.

He smiled and shook his head. 'I told you I came here to say goodbye.'

She shivered involuntarily at the memory.

'Well, you didn't give me a chance to explain. I wasn't sure that I would succeed but I had made up my mind to try — to try to say goodbye to Helen. I've done it. I've just been there to the churchyard.

'Things came back to me, little things she had said and done, things we'd shared. And I realised she was like a child to me always. I felt responsible for her and she relied on me. I loved her dearly, but it is only since I've known you that I've realised there is a different kind of love, a sharing, equal kind of love.

'You've forced me to see things I hadn't realised were there, things in myself and errors in my judgement. I know you're right.

'When people always look up to you it does put a lot of responsibility on you. Besides my father, you are the first person to challenge me.'

A smile crossed his face.

'Strange how I couldn't take it from him and yet from you it's entirely different.'

Then he was serious again. 'Because of this I can relax with you, knowing that whatever happens I could never have the power over you that I did over Helen.'

She knew what he meant, how he feared his own strength and the devastation it could cause, but she wondered if he knew how wrong he was. His hold over her would always be strong because of her love for him. But it didn't worry her one little bit for she trusted him implicitly.

'Where will we live?' he asked her, bringing her back to more practical considerations and she wondered if her plans for the theatre would now be possible.

He anticipated her thoughts and said, 'I suppose we'll be travelling quite a bit now that your new group is such a success.'

'You don't mind me continuing with it?' she asked.

'Of course not. I have my work, which is important to me. I certainly don't expect you to sit around looking beautiful, although I've no doubt you would be very good at it. No, Vanessa, I don't want you to change in any way. You'll have the whole Kilmorgan Estate behind you, and so long as I can always reach you I'll be content.'

'I'll never be far away,' she assured

him, not wanting ever to be farther away from him than she was at this moment.

Robert enfolded her in his strong arms and she relaxed against the deep warmth of his body.

She had never felt happier or more complete.

THE END

We do hope that you have enjoyed reading this large print book.

Did you know that all of our titles are available for purchase?

We publish a wide range of high quality large print books including:
Romances, Mysteries, Classics
General Fiction
Non Fiction and Westerns

Special interest titles available in large print are:
The Little Oxford Dictionary
Music Book, Song Book
Hymn Book, Service Book

Also available from us courtesy of Oxford University Press:
Young Readers' Dictionary
(large print edition)
Young Readers' Thesaurus
(large print edition)

For further information or a free brochure, please contact us at:
Ulverscroft Large Print Books Ltd.,
The Green, Bradgate Road, Anstey,
Leicester, LE7 7FU, England.
Tel: (00 44) 0116 236 4325
Fax: (00 44) 0116 234 0205

Other titles in the
Linford Romance Library:

VERA'S VENTURE

Anne Holman

World War II is over, but new problems confront Vera. Her wartime job ends, and her husband Geoff is invalided out of the army and needs work. With two young children they must leave their home and move into a rundown cottage in Norfolk. Geoff has taken an engineering job with the Fen River Board. And whilst the river banks desperately need strengthening, floods are threatening the flat Fenlands, and Vera must protect her family.

DARK FORTUNE

Susan Udy

A lottery win changes everything for Kate: even her closest friend resents her luck. So, she starts a new life elsewhere, keeping her fortune a secret. However, it's soon apparent that someone who knows the truth is subjecting her to a campaign of fear. Kate doesn't know which of her new friends to trust. Could it be Dan, her attractive neighbour; Irene, who swiftly befriends her; or the more disturbing Fergal? Or could it be someone from her past?

MOUNTAIN SHADOWS

Paula Williams

When Jenna Manning's mother dies, she makes a series of shocking discoveries. She learns that her mother had cut her out of her will . . . but then finds that, along with the thriller writer Luke Grantley, she's part-owner of the family's old home in Cumbria. Jenna decides to visit 'Brackwith' and finds the injured Luke in residence. But it's only after stumbling upon the truth about her father, that Jenna and Luke realise their lives have become completely entwined.

DREAMING OF LOVE

Fay Cunningham

Alice first meets Leo Grant late at night in the local supermarket. Unfortunately, she is wearing bunny pyjamas and a woolly hat — not exactly the outfit she would normally choose to impress a famous American author, particularly when he is with a gorgeous redhead. Lucy's five-year-old niece thinks Leo Grant is a prince in disguise, straight out of a storybook, and the mysterious redhead is hiding a deadly secret. Alice's world is about to get curiouser and curiouser . . .

A CHANCE ENCOUNTER

Margaret Mounsdon

When Grace Maxwell swerves to avoid a dog that runs out in front of her car, the near miss begins a chain of events that leads her to Daniel Stafford. At the college ball, Melissa Harper, Daniel's fiancée, had discovered Grace and Daniel kissing, and she had broken off their engagement . . . Grace now works as a vet's receptionist and to make matters worse Daniel takes over the practice. Then she learns Melissa Harper is back on the scene . . .

NOT AS A COWARD

Lillie Howard

Adele Price, after a sheltered Victorian upbringing with her kindly aunt and uncle in Wiltshire, longs for a challenge in life. Then she meets Philip Belvedere, and after a whirlwind courtship, they marry. Philip takes her back to Sadura, his home town in south-west India, and Adele is indeed challenged. The house is dominated by Philip's old ayah, and Philip's behaviour seems strange and deceitful. Meanwhile, it's David Baxter, the local doctor, who helps Adele to face her troubles . . .